BIT'S
Bliss

USA TODAY BESTSELLING AUTHOR
HEATHER SLADE

BIT'S BLISS

© 2024 Heather Slade

All rights reserved. No part of this book may be used or reproduced in any manner whatsoever without written permission, except in the case of brief quotations embodied in critical articles and reviews.

This book is a work of fiction. The names, characters, places and incidents are products of the writer's imagination or have been used fictitiously and are not to be construed as real. Any resemblance to persons, living or dead, actual events, locale or organizations is entirely coincidental.

979-8-88649-111-1

MORE FROM AUTHOR HEATHER SLADE

BUTLER RANCH
Kade's Worth
Brodie's Promise
Maddox's Truce
Naughton's Secret
Mercer's Vow
Kade's Return
Butler Ranch Christmas

WICKED WINEMAKERS
FIRST LABEL
Brix's Bid
Ridge's Release
Press' Passion
Zin's Sins
Tryst's Temptation

WICKED WINEMAKERS
SECOND LABEL
Beau's Beloved
Cru's Crush
Bit's Bliss
Coming Soon:
Snapper's Seduction
Kick's Kiss

ROARING FORK RANCH
Roaring Fork Wrangler
Coming Soon:
Roaring Fork Roughstock
Roaring Fork Rockstar
Roaring Fork Rooker
Roaring Fork Bridger

THE ROYAL AGENTS
OF MI6
Make Me Shiver
Drive Me Wilder
Feel My Pinch
Chase My Shadow
Find My Angel

K19 SECURITY
SOLUTIONS TEAM ONE
Razor's Edge
Gunner's Redemption
Mistletoe's Magic
Mantis' Desire
Dutch's Salvation

K19 SECURITY
SOLUTIONS TEAM TWO
Striker's Choice
Monk's Fire
Halo's Oath
Tackle's Honor
Onyx's Awakening

K19 SHADOW OPERATIONS
TEAM ONE
Code Name: Ranger
Code Name: Diesel
Code Name: Wasp
Code Name: Cowboy
Code Name: Mayhem

K19 ALLIED INTELLIGENCE
TEAM ONE
Code Name: Ares
Code Name: Cayman
Code Name: Poseidon
Code Name: Zeppelin
Code Name: Magnet

K19 ALLIED INTELLIGENCE
TEAM TWO
Code Name: Puck
Code Name: Michelangelo
Code Name: Typhon
Coming Soon:
Code Name: Hornet
Code Name: Reaper

PROTECTORS
UNDERCOVER
Undercover Agent
Undercover Emissary
Undercover Savior
Coming Soon:
Undercover Infidel
Undercover Assassin

THE INVINCIBLES
TEAM ONE
Code Name: Deck
Code Name: Edge
Code Name: Grinder
Code Name: Rile
Code Name: Smoke

THE INVINCIBLES
TEAM TWO
Code Name: Buck
Code Name: Irish
Code Name: Saint
Code Name: Hammer
Code Name: Rip

THE UNSTOPPABLES
TEAM ONE
Code Name: Fury
Code Name: Merried
Coming Soon:
Code Name: Vex
Code Name: Steel
Code Name: Jagger

COWBOYS OF
CRESTED BUTTE
A Cowboy Falls
A Cowboy's Dance
A Cowboy's Kiss
A Cowboy Stays
A Cowboy Wins

Table of Contents

Chapter 1 1
Chapter 2 9
Chapter 3 18
Chapter 4 27
Chapter 5 39
Chapter 6 48
Chapter 7 56
Chapter 8 72
Chapter 9 81
Chapter 10 94
Chapter 11 108
Chapter 12 124
Chapter 13 134
Chapter 14 143
Chapter 15 156
Chapter 16 171
Chapter 17 186
Chapter 18 195
Chapter 19 211
Chapter 20 219

Chapter 21 238
Chapter 22 249
Chapter 23 265
Chapter 24 274
Chapter 25 281
Chapter 26 287
Chapter 27 296
Chapter 28 305
Chapter 29 313
Chapter 30 318
Snapper's Seduction 323
About the Author 327

1
Bit

My sister told me to imagine everyone in the room was naked when I stepped out onto the stage as the last man being auctioned for a date as part of the Wicked Winemakers' Ball's bachelor auction.

While Alex was trying to be helpful, I wasn't as nervous as she assumed. In fact, part of me hoped no one would bid on my date. If that happened, it would be the last time she'd pressure me to do this.

As far as picturing anyone naked, there was one person in the room I wanted to imagine that way, *Eberly Warwick*. It would take more than two hands to count the number of reasons I shouldn't—*couldn't*—pursue anything beyond a professional relationship with her. The woman's wide-eyed innocence meant she was hands-off due to the dark desires someone like me not only preferred but needed.

Restraining myself around her was most difficult when we worked side by side at the parties we hosted in the original winery building on my family's property.

On her first day on her job as an event planner, I'd followed her as she looked around the space inside and out and jotted notes on a pad of paper.

"What did you write?" I asked when she stuck her pencil behind her ear and smiled.

"We'll call it the Los Caballeros Stonehouse and Gardens."

"We will?" I asked, taking in the sparse and mostly dead grass on every side of the building. "That might be misleading. Are you sure you don't want to call it the old winery building?"

"Close your eyes," she'd said.

Since, at that particular moment, I wanted her enough to willingly do whatever she asked of me, even bark like a dog, I squeezed them shut.

"Imagine the most beautiful gardens you've ever seen in your life."

"Okay."

"Where are they?"

"At the inn in Cambria."

"Right! That's perfect!"

I peeked through one eye, saw her writing something else on the pad, then shut it before she caught me.

"What are your favorite flowers?" she asked.

"I don't know. Roses, I guess."

"Also perfect. We'll use them on the wall in the front. Then, behind the building, we'll plant a kitchen garden, and on the side leading into the woods, we could build an enclosure and call it the secret garden. And here—"

"Eberly, can I open my eyes?"

Her simple touch on my arm sent white-hot desire coursing through my body, making me flinch.

"Sorry," she whispered.

My eyes scrunched as I studied her. Had I imagined the way her breath caught or the flush evident on her skin? What would the sweet Eberly do if I grabbed her wrists with one hand, pushed her up against the side of the building, spread her legs, eased my other hand beneath the short dress she wore, then under the panties I'd never let her wear if she were mine, and gave her pleasure like none she'd ever known?

As if sensing my plan, Eberly walked to the opposite side of the low wall encompassing the courtyard that led to the building's entrance. "Can you imagine this space with Eden climbers and ivy covering the stone?" she asked in a trembling voice. "Roses," she added when I didn't react.

"I can't," I responded.

"Can't what?"

"Imagine it." I was too unwilling to let go of the vision of her clinging to me as I toyed with her drenched sex.

"Of course you can!"

I shook my head.

She'd led me inside that day, and when she told me to picture a couple dancing in this room, I repeated that I couldn't. Not unless it was her and me, of course.

"Maybe this will help." She stood in front of me, then put one of my arms around her waist and her hand in my other. "Twirl me around the room," she said.

I stood in place, staring at her. Was she truly unaware of the way my aching cock yearned to be inside her?

"Okay, I'll do it," she said.

I was powerless to do anything but follow her lead as she spun us around and around until I felt dizzy. Halfway across the room, I took control like I always would with her. Easing the hand she'd put on her waist down slowly, I imagined how Eberly might respond if I let her see the side of me no one imagined existed.

I didn't doubt that most, including my own family, thought the attack that almost killed me had left me permanently concussed.

Nothing could be further from the truth. Instead, I lived in a state of high alert, seeing and hearing the slightest nuances of another person's words, their breathing patterns, and even their subtlest movements.

When my sister asked me to come up with an idea for a date to auction, an innocent day like that one I spent with Eberly, dancing under the twinkling lights, was all I could come up with.

"Ladies, you are in for a real treat tonight. For the very first time, you can bid on a date with my brother Trevino!"

I scanned the crowd until my eyes met Eberly's, stunned when, instead of looking away, she raised her chin and kept her gaze riveted on mine.

"Go ahead," Alex whispered with her hand over the mic.

I stepped forward and stopped at the stage's midpoint.

"Trevino has promised the winning bidder one of the most romantic dates we've ever had at the Wicked

Winemakers' Ball. First, a walk on Moonstone Beach, followed by a motorcycle ride—which, by the way, I didn't know he had—on See Canyon Road. When you arrive at Los Caballeros, you'll be swept away on horseback to the winery's Stonehouse and Gardens, where you'll enjoy a private dinner, followed by dancing under the twinkling lights."

Eberly smiled and let her gaze drop as if she knew my intent was to recreate the day I held her in my arms and we danced.

"Okay, ladies, who wants to start us off with an opening bid of a thousand dollars?"

Eberly raised her paddle. "I'll bid five."

"Five?" Alex asked.

"Thousand."

"Excellent! Let's start bidding at five thousand. Six thousand, anyone?"

I was disappointed that while other bidders raised their paddles, Eberly didn't, especially since she'd started it off.

"Going twice," I heard my sister say at the same time Eberly stood.

A hush came over the room as everyone waited for her to speak. "Twenty-five thousand."

"Sold!" Alex proclaimed without the customary countdown. "Well done, Bit," she said, slipping her arm through mine.

She was wrong. Nothing good would come from Eberly Warwick spending that amount of time alone with me. Of having her body pressed against mine as we sped through the hills of Paso Robles on my bike, or when my cock rested between the cheeks of her ass as we rode bareback from the Los Caballeros stables to the Stonehouse, where, if I allowed my fantasies to come to life, I'd feast on her body instead of the promised meal.

I shook my head, knowing I had no business going through with this. Instead, I'd cover Eberly's bid myself, then disappear for a while, like I always did when I felt the walls that hid my true thoughts and desires lowering enough that I might permit someone, like the woman I couldn't stop staring at, to see.

"Alex, I—" My voice froze, and every muscle in my body tensed when someone walking into the event center through a side door ripped my attention away from my bidder. He wore a tuxedo like the rest of the male guests in attendance, but I knew damned well he didn't belong here. When he scanned the room and stopped in the direction of Eberly's seat, my blood boiled.

"Trevino? What's wrong?" Alex asked as I removed my arm from hers, stepped forward, and jumped from the stage. As soon as our eyes met, he hurried outside.

"Trev, what the hell's going on?" hollered Brix, following when I rushed out the same door.

"Where the fuck did he go?" I shouted, spinning in a circle when I didn't see him or anyone else in the parking lot.

"Where did who go?" Brix asked, gripping my shoulder.

I jerked out of his grasp. "It was him. I know it was."

"Who?" he repeated.

It had been nearly a year to the day, but his was a face I'd never forget. "The *sonuvabitch* who tried to kill me."

2
Eberly

"What in the world was that about?" my father's date muttered under her breath. Her arms were folded, and she added an eye roll, seemingly for effect. I didn't respond. Unlike her, it wasn't that I was being rude. I wondered the same thing.

Like most everyone in the room, my eyes were riveted on the side door Trevino had rushed out of. When neither he nor his brother, who'd followed him, returned inside, the crowd eventually lost interest and resumed their chatter.

"Okay, everyone, bear with me. We have one more date to auction," Alex said from the stage. "You won't want to miss this," she added, tapping the microphone. She kept talking, but I couldn't focus on what she was saying, especially when Brix walked in alone.

I stood and intercepted him before he reached his table.

"Where's Trevino?" I asked.

"Hey, Eberly. Uh, I think he went home."

"What happened?"

Brix sighed and looked beyond me to his wife. He held up his index finger, and when she nodded, he led me away from the tables.

"You know about the incident in the caves, right?" he asked.

"Not exactly. Rumor was someone attacked him."

"Bit, err, Trevino, sometimes has flashbacks. Not that he did tonight." He hung his head. "Sorry. I'm not making sense. He thought he saw someone."

"Do you mean the guy who came in, then turned around and left?"

Brix's eyes opened wide. "You saw him too?"

"I didn't notice him until he was on his way out, and couldn't see his face. Like most everyone else, I saw Trevino's reaction when he jumped off the stage."

"Shit," he muttered, looking in the direction of the door that remained closed. "I can't leave Addison," he said more to himself than me. "Let me see if Snapper or Kick are around." He pulled his cell phone out of his pocket, then tapped the screen a few times and brought it to his ear.

"Hey, where are you?" He paused. "Can you head to Los Cab and check on Bit?" He paused a second time. "Yeah, right away. And can you tell him I was mistaken and I'm sorry?"

"Are you sure that's where he went?" I asked when he ended the call after thanking his brother. "Wait, never mind." Before I started working as an event planner at Los Caballeros, my profile, which included fingerprint, palm, and eye scans, had been entered into their security system. No doubt Brix already knew Trevino was home before he'd placed the call.

"I feel like a shithead," he muttered, more to himself than me for the second time. "I didn't see the guy," he added.

"I'm sure he understands."

Trevino's oldest brother studied me. "You bid a great deal of money for a date with him."

"It's a fundraiser," I murmured, knowing the question Brix was about to ask and wishing he wouldn't.

"Didn't I hear you were engaged—"

"No."

He raised a brow when I cut him off.

"We decided not to go through with it."

That wasn't exactly how it went. Tiernan, the man who was supposed to be my husband by now, hadn't discussed it with me. Instead, he'd sent my father.

One week ago today—the morning of our scheduled wedding—my dad had knocked on my bedroom door, asking if we could talk. When I told him to come in, he took my hand, pulled me to the bed, and we sat on the edge.

"I'm sorry, Eb. I know it's hard to imagine now, but in the long run, it's for the best," he began.

What should've come as a shock when he told me Tiernan had changed his mind and the wedding was off, hadn't. That in itself surprised me.

Sure, I was pissed, particularly since the man I was engaged to for over a year hadn't had the decency to break things off in person or even call to tell me himself. Deep inside, though, I was relieved.

"Did he say why?" I'd asked.

"He had a change of heart."

How many times had I felt the same way? Except, unlike him, I hadn't been brave enough to call it off.

"Right. If you don't mind, I'd like to be alone."

He let go of my hand, stood, and left the room.

"I'm sorry to hear that," I heard Brix say, tearing my thoughts from one of the most humiliating days of my life.

"Don't be. It was for the best."

After glancing over at the table where my father sat next to his latest paramour, currently talking his ear off, I decided to speak to the woman helping Alex with the auction, settle my bid, then leave.

"Excuse me," I said to Brix. I hadn't taken three steps when I was approached by the women who would've been my bridesmaids had there been a wedding.

"Oh my God, Eb. What was that about?" asked Isabel Van Orr. Like me, her mother had passed away a few years ago, and she and I had bonded over our losses. Admittedly, we hadn't been close prior to that despite our fathers being best friends, and knowing each other for most of our lives. There'd been several occasions when her concern for me felt unauthentic, as if under a facade, she took pleasure in my misfortune. Not just mine—everyone's.

"Are you okay?" the other woman, Justine Norman, asked. Her family was hosting the event this year at their winery.

"I'm fine."

Isabel folded her arms. "What is wrong with him anyway?"

My eyes met Justine's, and she rolled hers like my father's date had. Except I knew it wasn't meant for Trevino. We'd commiserated more than once about how judgmental Isabel could be.

"I, uh, need to take care of the bid payment. I'll talk to you later."

As I walked away, I saw Isabel raise a brow. I was sure Justine was about to get an earful either about Trevino or me, or maybe both of us.

"Hey, Eberly," said Saffron, the woman helping Alex with the event. I watched as she shuffled through a pile of papers. At one point, I'd thought about volunteering too, but the truth of the matter was Alexis Avila-Butler intimidated the hell out of me. Not only her. That so many people did had been one of many issues between Tiernan and me.

I was too young, too naive, too innocent, *too easily intimidated*. The irony was that no one made me feel less secure than he did. Not to mention, he'd never once gone much beyond kissing me. If my *innocence* bothered him so much, he'd had every opportunity to do something about my total lack of sexual experience.

It was one of hundreds of things I wished I could talk to my mom about. I often wondered what she would've thought of Tiernan had they met. Reflecting on our brief courtship, I knew she probably would've encouraged me to run far and fast in the opposite direction. It was a yardstick I should use in the future. What would my mom have thought? I knew how she felt about Trevino Avila.

"Out of all the brothers, he's my favorite," she'd said one day when we were at a wine industry event the family was hosting at Los Caballeros.

"Why?" I'd asked.

"I prefer the strong, silent type," she'd responded, winking. "Like your dad."

I shuddered, thinking about it. My father was a good man; I'd never doubted it. But even once I'd gotten to know Trevino better after I started working for him, I never would've said he was anything like my dad.

"Here it is," said Saffron, pulling a sheet from the pile. "The wiring instructions are at the bottom. We're asking donations be finalized within ten business days. If you need more time, let Alex or me know."

"No problem," I said, tucking the paper in my clutch.

"Hey, honey. I'm going to take Nancy home. See you at the house?" my dad approached and said.

"I might meet up with a friend."

"Sounds good. See you later," he said, waving behind him.

As I walked to my car in the parking lot, I felt as though I was being watched. There were plenty of people leaving like I was, and none seemed to be paying any attention to me. Still, the hair on my neck stood on end.

I gripped the car's door handle, which unlocked the driver's side, jumped in, and started the engine. After reversing out of the space, I drove to the closest exit and turned in the direction of Los Cab.

Given I'd just had one man end our engagement at the eleventh hour, part of me worried I'd gone too far, bidding for a date with Trevino, and that was at least one of the reasons he'd left without saying a word to me. Especially with the amount I paid.

Even if I hadn't gone so far as to bid on a date with him, our family always made a sizable donation to the charity the event supported. This was the first time I'd used my own money, though. Part of the trust fund my mother had set up for me shortly after I was born became mine once I graduated from college, and so far, I hadn't used much of it—apart from the wedding expenses I wasn't able to get refunded.

"Argh," I groaned out loud. Every time I thought about how Tiernan had treated me, I got angry. He was a misogynistic, condescending, controlling asshole who I was lucky to have out of my life.

The day I'd interviewed for the job at Los Caballeros, I felt an immediate, overwhelming attraction to Trevino. What kind of woman gets married when she has such strong feelings for someone else?

I wasn't stupid enough to think he'd ever feel the same way about me. But that wasn't the point. The attraction alone should've made me sit up and take stock of how I really felt about Tiernan. It wasn't a mistake I'd make again. In fact, *ever* getting married held zero appeal.

Maybe what I should do instead was find a man I liked enough, trusted enough, to *finally* have sex with. Again, I knew that wouldn't be Trevino, no matter how much money I paid to have the chance to spend time with him outside of work.

As I pulled through the gates of Los Caballeros, I made a decision. I'd let him off the hook by telling him my plan was to donate the money all along, and that I had no interest in actually going on the date.

3
Bit

I wasn't home twenty minutes before receiving an alert that my brother Salazar, who everyone called Snapper, had driven through Los Cab's main gate. Since I monitored the security feeds, I knew when everyone arrived and left.

When he pulled up to the guest cottage I'd made my home, I was already standing near the open front door.

"Hey, man. How was the ball?" he asked.

"Shy a couple of Avila brothers. Don't think you won't be hearing from Alex."

Snapper took the porch steps two at a time. "Anything of interest happen this year?" he asked when I waved him inside.

"Brix called you, didn't he?"

"He said you thought you saw someone."

"I didn't think it. He walked in the side door while I was still on stage."

"Who did?"

"The guy who tried to kill me."

"O'Donnell?"

I shook my head. "Grogan."

Snapper pulled out his cell and swiped the screen. "Couldn't have been either of them." He turned the phone around so I could see that both men were still in prison. "No one from FAIM or the Killeens will be eligible for parole for another ten years, at least."

Each "family" Snapper had mentioned proclaimed ties to the Irish Mafia, not that they acknowledged an affiliation.

Shortly after I was attacked as part of a kidnapping scheme, the two rival factions had been taken down by the organized-crime division of the FBI in what was the culmination of a five-year investigation.

Two hundred and fifty people in total were arrested and prosecuted, although I had no idea how many were from FAIM or from the Killeens. Most of the charges were drug-trafficking related, but the list of convictions included money laundering, witness retaliation, witness tampering, maintaining drug premises, illegal firearms possession, possession of drugs and drug paraphernalia, and finally, murder. A few received life sentences without parole, but most, as Snapper said, would be eligible in ten years.

"I'll never forget his eyes," I mumbled, looking at the image my brother had pulled up on the screen. I used my fingers to enlarge the mug shot. It was the color of his irises that stuck with me. They were amber, and when the light from the cave's sconces hit them, they'd glowed like cat eyes.

Snapper's brow was furrowed when I returned his phone. "They are an unusual color."

"Shared by less than five percent of the world's population."

"Is that right?"

I glared at him. I wouldn't have said it if it wasn't true.

"Could it have been the lighting in the room?"

I glared at him again, then went into the kitchen. "Want one?" I asked, holding up a can of non-alcoholic beer rather than the regular-strength one I was having.

"I'm good," he responded, making a face at the NA beer.

"You're driving," I muttered.

"Yeah. Also, not thirsty."

"What are you doing now?" I asked when he focused on something on his phone.

"Checking the security footage from Norman."

I wasn't surprised my brother had gotten his hands on the recordings so quickly. George Norman, whose winery hosted tonight's event, was close friends with our uncle, Tryst Avila. The two men had been members of a secret society called Los Caballeros, a brotherhood that had been in existence for several hundred years. My ancestors had established the branch in the US when they came to the country in the seventeen hundreds; at the same time, they gave the name to our family's winery.

All my brothers were *caballeros*. I'd joined a few weeks ago after Brix insisted I do in order to call an emergency meeting.

At the time, my next oldest sibling, Cru, was in Australia, visiting his fiancée, Daphne, who'd returned home after her father—a former *caballero*—had a stroke. The family's business, called Cullen House, operated out of Perth, Australia, and had started out in wine distribution. Over the years, they expanded exponentially and, now, owned a majority percentage of the larger wineries in the country. While Cru was there, he learned the chairman of the board of the multi-billion-dollar corporation, a man Daphne's father hadn't appointed, was attempting a hostile takeover.

Uncle Tryst, George Norman, and the eight other *caballeros viejos*, as they called themselves, had prevented the leveraged buyout and proved the now-former chairman was actually a corporate spy for Cullen House's biggest competitor.

Brix had been after me to become a *caballero* for years, saying it was my familial duty. My argument had always been that the Avila family was already well represented by him and our four other brothers.

Since no one other than those initiated into the organization was permitted to attend meetings, much less call them, he'd finally gotten what he wanted by forcing my hand.

"Is this who you saw?" Snapper asked, holding his phone out a second time.

The man maneuvered his body as he approached the door, and when he rushed away from it, he did it in such a way that it was impossible to see his face—a telltale sign of a criminal.

"That guy has to be six-foot-two or -three at least," Snapper commented. "Neither O'Donnell nor Grogan were that tall."

"I know what I saw," I said, rubbing my left temple when that side of my head started to throb. Severe migraines were a side effect of the hit I'd taken, one my doctors said would eventually diminish, but so far, it seemed like they grew more frequent.

When security alerts popped up on my brother's phone and mine, I figured it was Cru returning from the event. Instead, Eberly's profile appeared.

"Shit," I said under my breath, not surprised that she'd showed up. She was probably wondering what the fuck had happened since I took off within minutes of her bidding twenty-five grand for a date with me.

"What do you want to do, Bit?" Snapper asked.

"You can take off."

My brother squeezed my shoulder. "You sure?"

I jerked away from him, which made my head throb more. "I'm fine."

"I'll check in tomorrow. Oh, and Eberly arrived."

"Tell her to come in."

I heard the two of them talking as I flicked the lights off in the kitchen and living room. I'd started a fire as soon as I got home earlier, and it was bright enough to illuminate the space. I dumped the rest of my beer in the sink, then turned around to face Eberly when she walked in.

"Hey," I said, resting my hands on the counter. "Sorry about taking off like that."

"It's okay. Brix said you thought you saw someone."

"I was mistaken." I squeezed my eyes shut when the pain in my head got worse. When I opened them, she was standing beside me.

"What's wrong?" she asked.

"Migraine."

"Do you have a cold pack?"

"Yeah," I muttered, pointing to the fridge.

"Does that help more, or does heat?"

"Both." I couldn't decide which stunned me more; that she'd asked or that I answered.

She opened the freezer, pulled out the pack, then grabbed one of the cans of iced coffee I kept on hand from the refrigerator. She held it up. "Will this help?"

"Sometimes."

"Do you want to sit or lie down?"

I motioned to the living room, then held my hand out.

"Hang on. I want to wrap the pack in something, and I'll pour the coffee into a glass. Go sit. I'll only be a minute."

"You have experience with migraines?" I asked.

"My mom had them often when she was sick. What about heat?"

"Bedroom. There's a pad plugged in next to the bed."

She handed me the cold pack she'd wrapped in a towel and set the coffee on the table.

"Where does it help the most?" she asked when she returned with the heating pad.

"Shoulders. There's an outlet—"

"Shh. I've got this."

Truth was every movement—even talking—hurt. "Bed might be better," I said when I couldn't find a comfortable position on the sofa. "You don't have to stick around," I added when I realized she was following me.

"I'll help you get settled, then I'll go."

Eberly sat on the edge of the bed when I lay on my stomach. She pressed the cold pack against the left side of my head and draped the heating pad over my shoulders. I felt her hands move to the back of my neck, then her thumbs press on either side of the base of my skull while her fingers fanned and rested gently above them.

"Gates of consciousness," I whispered as I felt the tension in my neck and shoulders loosen from the pressure of her thumbs. It was the first time in the last year, when migraines plagued me sometimes several times a week, that anyone had recognized my pain or attempted to help me with it. More, I'd never permitted anyone to do so. "Thanks," I murmured.

"Shh," she soothed, and within seconds, I fell asleep.

I woke periodically when she'd shift position or switched out the cold packs. Each time, I wanted to tell her again that she could leave, but I couldn't bring myself to. Her touch was a balm like none I'd ever known.

When I opened my eyes sometime in the middle of the night, the pain was gone but Eberly wasn't. Her right hand still rested on the base of my skull, but her left arm propped her head up, and she was sound asleep. Rather than wake her, I let my gaze linger on her beautiful face. This would be the single time I would allow the woman to be in my bed, and I wasn't ready for it to end.

I rolled over when daylight streamed through the window. By then, Eberly was no longer beside me. No doubt she'd already gone home. I rubbed my neck where her hand had been, knowing her absence was for the best, but wishing it wasn't.

4

Eberly

My father's car wasn't in the garage when I pulled mine in, and while I breathed a sigh of relief, I remembered him saying he was dropping Nancy off and coming home.

Even if he had been here, it wasn't like he'd get up and ask me why I was rolling in at four in the morning, in the same way, when I'd see him later, I wouldn't ask where he'd been.

I was eighteen when my mother died, and that fall, I left for college in the northern part of the state. Sometimes, I came home for breaks, but more often, I traveled with friends. When I graduated, I hadn't planned to be home longer than a visit.

Shortly after, though, I'd started dating Tiernan. It made no sense to get a place of my own since, early on, he'd made it clear his intention was for us to marry. Once we were, he said I'd move in with him. That he hadn't wanted me to until then, even after we were engaged, should've bothered me more than it did. Or worried me. Instead, it hadn't fazed me in the slightest.

Once upstairs, I wriggled out of the ridiculously uncomfortable dress I'd been wearing for close to ten hours, removed my makeup, and got in the shower, letting the hot water soothe my sore shoulders.

As much as I hadn't wanted to leave Trevino, I knew he'd be uncomfortable if he woke up and I was still there. As it was, I'd lingered too long. He'd slept most of the night, which based on my experience with my mom, meant his migraine pain had eased.

So why had I stayed? Because I knew Monday morning, when I showed up for work, Trevino would put the distance between us that I'd grown accustomed to. That would be if I saw him at all. More than likely, he'd avoid me for as long as he could, and that would be okay too. I had work to do, mostly getting the gardens ready for spring, when the event business would pick up again.

Soon, it would be time to plant the bulbs that would grow and bloom in March and April, but for the time being, there were several native plants and cool-season annuals I could get started.

Being outdoors, even when the weather was chilly, was a boon for my soul. Planting flowers and vegetables was something my mother and I had done together from the time I was a child. Dad reminded us more than once that we had several people on the vineyard payroll who could do it for us. Mom and I got to the point where we ignored him rather than mention again how much we enjoyed doing it. Trevino had said the same thing to me the day I showed up dressed to spend my shift "playing in the dirt," as I'd told him.

"Do you want some help?" he'd asked.

I'd almost told him I'd love it—thinking he was offering. Fortunately, I'd bit my tongue since he added he could send some of the guys who worked in the vines over to help me plant.

"I like doing it myself," I'd said instead.

"Understood," he'd responded, leaving me on my own for the rest of the day.

Deciding I probably wouldn't sleep, I went downstairs, made a cup of coffee, and dug out the sketches I'd done of the grounds around the old winery, as Trevino called it.

When I raised my head and saw it was close to nine, I was stunned. First, by how much time I'd lost track of but also that my dad still wasn't home.

"I guess he's entitled," I muttered to myself, closing my sketchpad. I was about to leave the kitchen when the landline rang—something it rarely did since its only purpose was to buzz someone in the front gate. I thought about not picking up, but did anyway.

"Hello?" I answered.

"Eberly? It's Trevino. I'm out front. Can you open the gate?"

"Um, sure," I said, trying to remember how to do it. "Hang on one sec."

"There should be a code."

"Right. Of course." I hit the side of my head with my palm. How could I have forgotten? It was my damn birthday. I pressed the corresponding keys on the phone and, seconds later, heard the gate opening.

I ran my hand over my hair and glanced at my reflection. At least I'd combed it after getting out of the shower, and while I wasn't wearing pajamas, I hadn't bothered putting a bra on when I donned my favorite sweatpants and T-shirt. I folded my arms in front of me, then opened the door, waving when Trevino pulled in and parked.

"Good morning," I said when he got out of his truck. I'd never told him, but I loved it. I didn't know enough about vehicles to have any idea how old it was or even what kind. It was green and white and sat high enough that someone my size would probably need a footstool to get in.

"Mornin', Eberly."

"It looks as though you're feeling better."

"Thanks to you," he said, stepping closer.

"Do you want to come in?"

"Are you in the middle of something?"

"I was thinking about making breakfast," I lied. "Want to join me?"

He hesitated and looked down at his feet. "I probably shouldn't."

"Sure, um, of course. So, why'd you come by?"

His eyes met mine. "I didn't say no."

"Oh, uh, okay." I spun around and went inside; he was right behind me. "Coffee?" I asked.

"Do you have decaf?" he asked.

I pointed to the selection of pods we kept in a basket next to the smaller of our two coffeemakers.

"This one's good," he said, choosing one. "I can do it," he added rather than hand it to me. "What are you making?" he asked while I pulled things out of the refrigerator.

"Breakfast tacos?"

"Are you asking or telling?"

"Err, asking?"

"I'm not picky."

"Tacos it is."

"I'd offer to help, but I'd be in the way."

I cooked often, whether it was for myself, for me and my dad, or for friends I had over, so there was no reason I should be nervous making something so simple. Except I was. Shaking, in fact. "Why are you here, Trevino?" I asked, glancing over my shoulder to see him pull a stool at the counter and sit down.

"To apologize."

I broke several eggs into a bowl and whisked them. "What for?"

"First, running out on you rather than thanking you for bidding on me. Alex probably worried no one would."

"It wasn't me alone."

"Yeah, but you paid a lot of money. That was nice of you."

I'd tell him being *nice* had nothing to do with it. It was the opposite. Yeah, I knew nothing romantic would come of our date. Still, a girl could dream.

"You said, first. Was there something else?"

"You took care of me."

I added chorizo, then poured the egg mixture into a pan. "Are you apologizing for it?"

He shook his head. "I shouldn't have let you."

I turned up the heat under the eggs and moved them around the pan with more force than was necessary. So, I set the spatula down, put a hand on my hip, and turned to face him. "You could thank me."

His eyes bored into mine.

I shook my head. "Sorry. I shouldn't have said that."

He stood and walked in my direction. When it looked as though he didn't intend to stop, I took a couple of steps backward until I was up against the refrigerator.

Trevino stood as close to me as he could without making physical contact. "I shouldn't be here."

I raised my chin. "Why not?"

He touched the side of my face with the tip of his finger. "When you don't have makeup on, you look like a kid."

I bristled.

His finger trailed down my neck. "You didn't care for that."

"Would you?" My voice shook, making me sound more like the kid he'd called me.

He leaned forward, and the warmth of his breath near my ear tickled. "I'm older than you are, so I can't say it would bother me." He took a deep breath. "I like that, by the way. A lot."

My shoulders tightened. "That I look like a child?"

He leaned away slightly. "I said you look like a kid, not a child. And no, that isn't it."

"What, then?"

"You got mad at me."

I shook my head, but when I tried to scoot around him, he bracketed me with his arms.

"The eggs will burn."

He glanced over his shoulder and turned the heat off, then leaned into me so our bodies were flush.

"Why do you want me to be mad at you?" My voice had gone from shaky to breathy.

"I didn't say that either. I said I liked it that you did."

His hardness resting against my thighs pulsed when he lowered his hand to my bottom and squeezed.

While I'd thought about being with Trevino, it was never this way. What he was doing far exceeded my imagination. I shuddered when he squeezed a second time.

He brushed my lips with his but didn't kiss me. "I shouldn't be here," he repeated.

I tensed when I heard another vehicle pulling in. "My dad's home."

Trevino took a step away, then relit the burner under the eggs. "Finish making breakfast."

He was seated at the counter by the time my father came in. I still hadn't moved.

"Hey, Trev," my dad said to him before walking over to kiss my cheek. "What are you making?" he motioned to the stove.

"Breakfast tacos."

"Yum. Too bad I already ate."

I stopped myself from saying they weren't for him anyway.

"Okay, kids, enjoy."

Kids? God, I was beginning to hate the word.

I moved the eggs and chorizo around in the pan, lowered the heat, then sprinkled cheese on top. As I wrapped the tortillas in a damp paper towel and stuck them in the drawer microwave, I looked up at Trevino for the first time since my dad left the kitchen.

"What?" I said when his eyes scrunched.

"Why does being called a kid bother you so much?"

I took a knife out of the drawer and plunged it into an avocado. "I don't know. Maybe it's because I'm a twenty-three-year-old woman."

"Twenty-three?"

"You hired me. I assumed you knew my age."

"I didn't pay attention."

"Now, you know."

"That you're not a kid?"

"That's right." I opened the microwave, put two tortillas on a plate, then took it to the stove to add the eggs. "Do you want hot sauce?" I asked, setting it and the smaller plate where I'd put avocado slices in front of him.

"Yes, please."

His eyes widened when I set it down harder than I meant to.

"Sorry," I mumbled.

"You will be," he said under his breath.

My mouth gaped. "What does that mean?"

"You'll see."

I put both hands on my hips. "What will you do, fire me?"

He laughed and shook his head. "No, Eberly. I won't be firing you."

"What, then?"

He took a bite of his taco, then wiped his mouth with the cloth napkin I'd set next to his plate. "Don't ask questions you might not care for the answers to."

"Other than taking my job away, I can't imagine anything you'd do that I wouldn't."

He took another bite and raised a brow. "I bet you could if you tried."

"So, um, why do your brothers call you Bit?" I stammered in an awkward attempt to change the subject.

He wiped his mouth again and grinned. "Because they were all bigger than me."

My eyes opened wide, and he chuckled.

"It's true. I was a late bloomer."

I turned around to plate a taco for myself, not that I had much of an appetite. "You more than made up for it," I said under my breath, sighing before walking around the island to sit next to him. I'd just hoisted myself up on a stool when he spun it so I faced him, then spread my legs.

"I *should* fire you, you know?"

I looked down at his hands resting on my thighs, right above my knees. "Why?"

"As soon as I put my hands on you, I crossed a line."

I stared him down, unable to guess what he'd do next. Would he inch his fingers up my legs, or would he restrain himself? Instead of doing either, he squeezed my flexed muscles.

"Powerful. I like that."

I nearly whimpered when he released me and turned his body away from mine.

"Be careful what you wish for, Eberly. You might not like it as much as you think you will." He stood and took his plate to the sink. "See ya Monday," he said as I watched him walk out the same door he'd come in.

5
Bit

The drive from Eberly's to Los Cab was too short to assuage my overwhelming itch to get the hell out of town. Disappearing is what I did best, and it had started long before I was attacked in the wine caves.

It was the reason I hadn't agreed to join Los Caballeros or even work in our family's vineyards or winery. No responsibilities meant no one expected me to show up at a certain place at a specified time.

Once I reached the ranch's main gate, I forced myself to pull my truck through, then drove up and parked in front of the cottage where I'd been living for the last few months—far longer than I'd intended to.

So how in the fuck had I gotten here? By making the mistake of stopping in to see my brother Cru to let him know I was heading out of town.

I couldn't say it was his fault that I'd ended up staying. If anyone was to blame, it was our oldest sibling, Brix.

When he decided he was finished running the family business, he'd essentially dumped the bulk of it on Cru's shoulders. He'd gone from second-label winemaker to handling both it and the first-label varietals, and he'd also become the de facto vineyard manager.

Then again, when our father died suddenly when Brix was twenty-eight, hadn't the same thing happened to him? Brix had been expected to take over the management of the family's estate and business whether he wanted to or not. While I might agree he deserved to step away, had anyone asked my opinion—which no one ever did—I would let them know I didn't care for the way it had been at Cru's expense.

Whether he realized it or not, Cru was more similar to our dad, both in looks and demeanor, than the rest of us. My fear that he'd also suffer the same physical ailments that led to my father's premature death was what had instigated my decision to remain on my family's property for what was supposed to be a few days.

Then Cru had hired Daphne Cullen to take over the second label. My plan was to ensure that—unlike me, albeit for entirely different reasons—he'd be able to relinquish control of producing the wines that had been his responsibility for years.

Sheer boredom had led me to wander the estate that day, so many months ago, when I stumbled upon the old winery that was almost entirely camouflaged by overgrown vegetation. I remembered my father saying our production levels had outgrown the facility before I was even born. He'd probably intended to rip it down someday. It was one on a long list of things he'd wanted to do but hadn't gotten around to when his life was cut tragically short at the age of fifty-two.

I was still sitting in my truck when I glanced in the rearview mirror and saw Cru approaching.

"Everything okay?" he asked when I opened the door and got out.

"Fine. You?"

"Never better."

"Yeah?" I motioned for him to follow me inside.

"I guess you didn't hear what happened last night."

My breath caught. "What do you mean?"

"Daphne showed up. Which reminds me, where'd you run off to?"

"I had something to take care of. So, Daph's here?"

Cru beamed. "She was a late entry into the auction. First bachelorette."

"Wow. I had no idea."

"Best surprise of my life. Anyway, you were up and out of here early."

"Yeah," I muttered under my breath. I wasn't in the habit of explaining my comings and goings to anyone, and I wasn't about to start.

Cru's eyes scrunched, and he studied me.

"Something else you need?" I asked.

"Nah. I came by to let you know Daphne's here." He hesitated as though he expected me to say something else. When I didn't, he added, "I guess I'll catch you later, then."

I waited until he was gone before leaving as well. Rather than getting in my truck, I took the pathway to the old winery and went inside. Everything looked the same as when I was last here. Was that yesterday? Why, in less than twenty-four hours, did it feel so different?

Because it was, and this time, there'd be no undoing the damage I'd done by putting my hands on someone who worked for me. My only recourse now was to keep it from getting worse, and that meant staying the hell away from Eberly Warwick.

"Hey. Glad I found you," said Brix.

What the fuck? First, Snapper had stopped by last night, then Cru earlier, now Brix. Would I receive a visit from each of my siblings before the day's end?

He looked around the room, then stepped up to the tasting bar. "The place looks incredible."

"What do you want?"

"It's about Eberly. At least indirectly."

"I plan to cover her bid."

Brix pulled out a stool and took a seat. "I guess you've already heard."

"Heard what?"

"About their winery closing."

I went behind the bar, pulled a bottle from the shelves below, opened it, and poured two glasses. "I don't know what you're talking about."

"Last night, after you took off and I went inside, Eberly approached me. I was stunned to hear her engagement had been called off, and when I mentioned it to Tryst, he said he'd feared something like that would happen."

I rubbed my left temple out of habit, not that I felt a migraine coming on, although trying to follow whatever the hell Brix was talking about might give me one.

"Is this about the winery closing or her getting married?"

"Both."

I took a long drink from my glass and set it down. "Get to the fucking point."

He chuckled. "Same ol' Bit."

I opened my mouth to tell him to fuck off, but shut it when he held up a hand. "As I'm sure you know, the demand for wine has fallen off dramatically while the number of hectares being planted worldwide has doubled every year for the last five."

"I'm aware."

"Most of us in this region reacted early on by allowing certain varietals to remain dormant. And, ironically, the outbreak of Botrytis bunch rot this year had helped us more than it hurt. Not everyone in the valley fared as well as we did. Namely, Eberly Winery."

That Malcolm and Belinda Warwick had named their winery for their daughter made referencing it as confusing as our family's estate being called Los Caballeros.

"About eight months ago, Warwick made the decision to merge with the Wine Consortium. He wasn't alone. Many smaller producers, both here and in Napa, did the same when they realized how severe their losses might be. Within a week of the merger finalizing, the WC went public."

I'd heard of the consortium but only in passing. Given Los Cab was one of the largest producers in the State of California, we'd have no reason to join them.

"In last week's quarterly industry report, the WC alluded to the possibility that as much as half a million tons of grapes from their holdings would be left hanging this year."

My eyes opened wide.

"Subsequently, shares that were trading at upwards of ten dollars have plummeted. They are now worth less than ten cents."

This could go one of two ways. Either Warwick had dumped his stock prior to the announcement, in which case he'd be investigated for insider trading, or he'd lost everything.

"Are you saying Eberly bid with money she doesn't have?"

"I don't know for certain."

"As I said, I'll take care of it. Anything else?"

"Rumor is her former fiancé may have played a significant role in Malcolm's decision to merge with the WC."

"I'll get in touch with Alex about the bid." As far as what role Eberly's ex had played, it wasn't any of my business. More, I didn't give a shit.

Brix finished the wine in his glass and stood. He was almost to the door when he turned around. "Why are you covering her bid if you weren't aware of her father's financial situation?"

"Because I want to." I stuck the cork in the unfinished bottle and picked up both our glasses. "See ya, Brix."

"Right. See ya, Bit."

I hung out for a few minutes after he left, looking at what had been transformed from a dirty, dilapidated building slated for a wrecking ball to amazing. While I'd done my part, it was Eberly's touch that transformed it into something magical.

After shutting off the twinkling lights overhead that I'd turned on when I came in, I stepped outside and locked the door. As I walked past the roses that had been planted at the base of the stone wall, I saw a bloom I hadn't noticed before. Rather than pink, like Eberly had told me the flowers would be, this one was pure white. I reached for it but caught a thorn instead. When I pulled my hand away, drops of blood landed on the pristine petal, ruining its beauty in the same way I would Eberly if I let her get too close.

6

Eberly

After cleaning up the kitchen, I made another cup of coffee, went outside, and walked around the garden. On cloud-free days especially, I felt my mother's presence all around me. It was as though the sun's rays wrapped me in the same warmth her hugs always had. There were times when I missed her so much it was hard to breathe.

I longed to talk to her about Trevino. About how his visit this morning had confused me and how being close to him had made me feel as though my heart would beat out of my chest.

"Be careful what you wish for, Eberly. You might not like it as much as you think you will," he'd said right before leaving. I couldn't stop myself, though. I wanted his hands, his lips, his tongue on me and to feel his hardness between my legs. I meant it when I said I couldn't imagine anything he'd do to me that I wouldn't like. I craved the darkness I sensed just beneath the surface of everything he said and did in the same way a moth couldn't stay away from a flame.

I spent the rest of the morning and most of the afternoon pulling weeds and pruning the plants I'd neglected since I started working for Trevino.

When I heard a loud crash coming from inside the house, I flinched. Before I could get to my feet to see what had happened, my father stormed out the kitchen door.

"I warned you not to involve her. I have no control over the money left to her, and what's more, I'd sooner die than let you get your hands on it or her," he shouted into his phone. "You come near her again, and I'll end you. Do you fucking understand me?"

Those were the last words I heard him say before he got in his car and sped off, throwing gravel from the drive onto the lawn where I sat. I lowered my head, and when I raised it, he was long gone.

I'd left my cell phone inside and went in to grab it, hoping he'd left a message as to where he was going. When I didn't see one, I checked his study.

Papers were strewn everywhere, and when I knelt down to pick them up, I saw evidence of the crash I'd heard. A bronze sphere that usually sat on his desk was on the floor, and right above it, a large oval mirror was shattered. A glass vase that sat beneath it had also broken into several pieces that were scattered on the floor. I made my way over to his desk, careful not to step on the shards of glass, and picked up an envelope that had been torn open but sat face down. The return address was from a bank whose name I recognized and inside was a letter. My hand shook as I unfolded it, and I gasped when I read what it contained.

Unless an ungodly sum of money was paid by the end of the day tomorrow, our house would go into foreclosure. Was it even worth the amount they were demanding?

I sat in my dad's chair, still holding the letter, and called his cell. When it rang several times, then went to voicemail, I sent an urgent text, asking him to get in touch with me as soon as possible.

When I still hadn't heard from him by early evening, I called Baron Van Orr, Isabel's father and my dad's best friend. He apologized but said they hadn't spoken in several weeks. That in itself was troubling.

I couldn't think of anyone else to call and ask if they'd seen or heard from him other than Nancy, but I didn't have her number.

I stayed in the same place, hardly moving except to breathe, until after the sun had set.

I must have drifted to sleep, but woke when the landline rang. I checked the time and saw it was a few minutes after ten, and since my dad obviously still wasn't home, I ignored it. I'd seen enough slasher movies to imagine the ways my answering it could go wrong.

When it rang a second, third, fourth, then fifth time, I started to get freaked out. I slid from the chair to the floor and called the one person I could think of other than my father, who still wasn't picking up.

Trevino answered on the first ring. "Eberly? What's wrong?"

"My dad is gone. He left this afternoon, and I can't reach him." When the landline rang again, I squeezed my eyes shut and put my finger in my other ear. "I think someone is at the gate. I don't know what to do."

"Where are you now?" he asked.

"Home."

"Where specifically?"

"In my dad's study. It's on the first floor, across from the stairs."

"Does the house have an alarm system?"

"Yes, but it isn't on." I felt like such an idiot. Why hadn't I set it? I knew better.

"Can you arm it from where you're at?"

"N-n-no," I stammered.

"I'm going to put you on hold and call law enforcement. Don't hang up, okay?"

"Okay."

"Eberly? You still there?" he asked less than a minute later.

"Yes."

"I'm on my way, and so is the sheriff. He said he has the emergency code to let himself in the gate. I'll stay on the line with you, though."

"Okay," I repeated.

The landline rang twice more, but when I could hear sirens in the distance, it abruptly stopped.

"Hang tight. I'm on your road and can see the squad cars arriving now. Stay where you are. I'll come to you."

I could hear multiple vehicles pulling in and saw flashing red and blue lights. "The, um, door you came in earlier is unlocked."

His voice was muffled as though he'd put his hand over the mic, but I could still hear him cursing as he entered.

"Eberly? Are you in here?" he asked from the hallway outside the study.

"Yes, by the desk, but be careful. There's broken glass."

In what felt like less than a heartbeat, he lifted me in his arms and carried me out of the room and straight to his truck.

"We've got this, Trev. Get Eberly out of here," one of the deputies hollered when we rushed past him.

Without responding, he opened the driver's door, set me on the bench seat, and climbed in after me. When I scooted to the passenger side, he pulled me back next to him.

"Thank you for coming. I didn't know who else to call." I put my head in my hands. "Although I guess I could've called the sheriff myself."

"You did the right thing by calling me first," he said as he turned the truck around and drove out the open gate. "Tomorrow—not tonight—we're gonna talk about how much trouble you're in. For now, you're safe and you're with me, and that's what matters."

My eyes opened wide. I was in *trouble*?

"I'm sorry. I'm worried about my dad. Before he left, I heard him on the phone, shouting at whoever he was talking to. Then I found a letter from the bank threatening foreclosure."

His eyes scrunched, but he didn't appear surprised. "Did you know?"

"I heard a rumor earlier today, and to put your mind at ease, you don't have to worry about the auction bid. I took care of it."

My cheeks flamed. "I don't understand what's going on."

He drove through the Los Caballeros' gate, pulled up in front of his cottage, and parked. "As I said, we'll talk more tomorrow. For now, we both need some rest."

"That's when the bank is foreclosing."

"Another thing we'll address in the morning." Trevino got out and, when I scooted to the edge of the seat, put his hands on my waist and lowered me to the ground.

"You know where the bedroom is. Get yourself settled, and I'll join you in a few minutes," he said once we were inside.

"Um, okay."

"Eberly?"

I'd taken two steps, but stopped. "Yeah?"

"The same thing that happened last night will happen again tonight. The only difference is that, instead of you taking care of me, I'm gonna take care of you. Okay?"

"Okay," I responded without turning around.

"Eberly?" he repeated.

"Yes?"

"Look at me."

When I faced him, he closed the distance between us and took both my hands in his. "You can trust me."

"I know."

I entered the bedroom, toed off my shoes, and lay on the right side of the bed like I had last night. A few minutes later, Trevino came in.

"Get under the covers."

"I'll be okay."

He leaned forward and put his hands on the edge of the bed. "Eberly, I told you to get under the covers." There was enough light streaming in from the kitchen for me to see the look on his face.

"Yes, sir," I teased. As soon as I said the words, his expression changed.

He stood upright, and his eyes scrunched. "Go to sleep," he said as he walked out the bedroom door and closed it behind him.

7
Bit

I wasn't much of a drinker other than beer or wine, but the situation with the woman now lying in my bed warranted something stronger. I reached into the cabinet, pulled out a bottle of whiskey, and filled a third of a glass. I plopped a couple of ice cubes in it, then sat on the sofa in the living room.

It was close to eleven, and as wired as I felt, I probably wouldn't sleep much tonight.

I rubbed my left temple, again out of habit rather than because I felt a migraine coming on, rested against the sofa and thought about Eberly. While I'd said we wouldn't talk until morning, when we did, she'd be getting an earful.

First, why hadn't she put the alarm in "home" mode when her father hadn't returned? Even if he had, he knew how to disarm it. Then, when she told me the kitchen door was unlocked, I'd wanted to march into her father's study and put her over my knee. As if she wasn't scared enough. Showing her that side of myself would've terrified someone like her.

I leaned forward and put my head in my hands. For the second time in less than twenty-four hours, I itched to run. It didn't matter where or how far; I just had to get the hell out of here before I did something I knew I'd regret. Like walk into that bedroom and show Eberly exactly what it did to me when she called me *sir*. I was still rock hard and would stay that way if I kept thinking about it.

"Trevino?"

I sat up but didn't look in her direction. "Go to bed, Eberly."

"Will you at least tell me what I did to make you so angry?"

"I'm not angry. Now, *go to bed*," I repeated.

I felt her walking toward me as much as heard her. Every step she took sent my desire skyrocketing.

"I told you we aren't talking tonight."

When she stood in front of me, I tried so damn hard not to look, but when had I ever been able to stop myself when it came to her? I found every excuse to visit the old winery, to spend a few minutes staring at her.

"Please look at me," she begged.

Her words threatened to shatter every ounce of restraint I possessed, then when my gaze traveled the length of her body, I knew resisting her would be a losing battle. She still had on the same sweatshirt she wore earlier, but had removed her jeans, exposing her long, sexy-as-fuck legs.

My eyes bored into hers. "You're playing with fire, little girl."

"I'm not a little girl, and I'm not a kid."

I sprung off the sofa as much as stood, stalked around the table, and backed her up against the opposite wall. I captured both her wrists in one hand and held them above her head before leaning my body into hers. "Is that right? How do you explain your behavior tonight?"

Her eyes were wide. "You're right. I shouldn't have called you." She tried to wriggle from my grasp, but I held her in place with my free hand on her waist.

"That is the *only* smart thing you did. Not setting the alarm, not locking the fucking kitchen door, and not staying in my bedroom like I told you to are the things you did that put yourself at risk."

Our mouths were close enough to kiss, but I couldn't allow it to happen.

"How is coming out of the bedroom putting myself at risk?" Her voice was breathy and deep, her pupils were dilated to the point where there was no visible color, and her hardened nipples poked against my chest even through her sweatshirt.

Worse, I could smell her desire, and it was driving me mad. "I am not the man for you, Eberly," I said, brushing her lips with mine like I had earlier. "I'm warning you. Do as I say and save us both."

She raised herself on her tiptoes, dragging her nipples against my chest, and brought her mouth to my ear. "I don't want to be saved." She trailed her lips from there to the corner of my mouth.

I moved the hand holding her still from her waist to her neck. "I'm giving you one more chance. I'll let you go, and when I do, I want you to march that sweet ass into the bedroom, and once you're there, lock the fucking door."

When I released her hands, she grabbed my wrist. "No," she said right before crashing her mouth into mine. I angled my head and thrust my tongue between her lips that would soon be swollen from our lack of restraint. "Consider yourself warned."

I grabbed the bottom of her sweatshirt and pushed it up as she pulled it over her head. "If you don't get this off, I'll tear it from your body. Jesus," I moaned, covering her bare breasts with my hands, kneading her flesh before bringing my mouth to one nipple, then the other. Her whimpers of pleasure spurred me on, and when her fingernails dug into the flesh of my wrist, I thought maybe she'd orgasm from breast play alone. But something felt off. I raised my head and studied her.

"Eberly, look at me."

When she opened her eyes, they darted between mine.

"Tell me what you're thinking."

The shake of her head was almost imperceptible.

"Am I hurting you?"

She squeezed her eyes shut and lowered her head. "No. That isn't it."

I put my hands on either side of her face. "What is it, then?"

"I'm, um, not sure what to do."

Closing my eyes, like she had, when the meaning of what she was saying hit me, I looked up at the ceiling, then down at her.

"I'm sorry—"

I stopped Eberly's words with a kiss, put one arm behind her knees, lifted her in my arms, and carried her into the bedroom. With one hand, I moved the blanket and sheet out of my way, then rested her body on the bed. "Take off your panties," I said as I removed my own clothes.

When we were both naked, I lay beside her and gathered her near. I held her close, stroking her hair with one hand while trailing my fingers down her arm with the other.

"Trevino, are we going to—"

"Shh," I soothed. "All we'll do tonight is sleep in each other's arms."

When she took a breath as if she was about to say something more, I kissed her again.

"Sleep, little dove. I'll still be here when you wake up. I promise."

While Eberly eventually slept, I lay awake as thoughts raced through my head. The first thing I should be considering was how to revert to a purely professional relationship between us after holding her naked in my arms, but I pushed that aside. Now that I knew how perfectly our bodies fit together, there'd be no resisting touching her in every way she'd let me.

As far as her father's whereabouts, the logical explanation was that he was holed up with the woman he'd brought to the ball last night. Except, why wouldn't Eberly have thought of that?

My next question was who had been trying to gain access to her front gate so late at night and why had they left right before the sheriff arrived?

Then again, anyone with nefarious intentions would hardly call from the gate to be admitted. They'd sneak in some other way. A peripheral look at the Warwick security system told me it was antiquated.

After making contact with Eberly's father, the next most urgent matter was the bank threatening foreclosure. Depending on the amount they required to delay the action, that should be easily solved. At least temporarily.

However, if the Warwicks' financial issues were so bad that it had gotten this far, how would they come up with *any* sum of money?

While none of this was my damn business, Eberly needed help and she'd come to me for it. Regardless of how wrong a sexual relationship between us would be, I could still be her friend.

Right. Even when her naked body pressed against mine was a memory, I could live to be a hundred and never forget how good it felt.

She rolled to her side, so her back was to my front, giving me the perfect opportunity to relinquish my hold on her. Instead, I rolled too, leaving my rigid cock nowhere to settle other than between the cheeks of her pert ass.

When I opened my eyes, the rosy hues of dawn streamed in through the window and Eberly was no longer beside me. I sat up, relieved when I heard her soft footfalls outside the bedroom door.

Given I was typically a light sleeper, I was surprised she'd managed to get up without waking me. But hadn't I slept better than I had in years two nights ago, when she'd soothed the pain of my migraine?

I rolled out of bed, pulled a pair of sweats out of a dresser drawer, and spotted her black lace panties lying on the floor. "Fuck," I muttered when the sight of them made me instantly hard—something the pants I intended to wear wouldn't hide. Instead, I grabbed a pair of jeans, not that they were much better.

"You're up early," I said, opening the door, then wishing I hadn't. She stood in my kitchen, wearing the shirt I'd had on last night and—considering I'd spotted her panties—nothing else.

She turned around and rested her behind against the counter. "I'm sorry if I woke you."

"You didn't."

She looked away.

"What's goin' on, Eberly?"

She raised both hands and covered her face. "I feel like an idiot."

I stepped closer, grabbed her wrists, then lowered them. "There's no reason you should."

"I'm sorry about, you know, last night."

I grinned. "Yeah? Which part? Cause if it's what happened in my living room, I can tell you I'm not." What was I doing? *Jesus.* Every word I spoke was in direct conflict with my *just* telling myself to be her friend and nothing else.

"I'm not exactly the seductress I may have appeared to be." She squeezed her eyes shut. "See? Even now, I sound like an idiot."

I rested my forehead against hers and tightened my grip on her wrists. "Stop it."

"I should, um, probably get home in case my dad showed up or shows up." She looked up so I could see her eyes. "I really need to figure out what to do about our house."

"Have you tried calling him?"

"It rang a few times, then went to voicemail."

I let go of her wrists. "I'll be happy to take you home so you can pick up a few things, but I don't think it's a good idea for you to stay there alone. Not until we find out who was at the gate last night. I'll call Vader, err, the sheriff later and see what they know."

"I have to talk to someone at the bank today. I figured it would be better to show up in person rather than calling."

"Good plan. What else has your mind racing this morning?"

She smiled for the first time since I opened the bedroom door and joined her in the kitchen. "Coffee?"

I chuckled. "That, I can help with." I walked to the cupboard where I kept a French press, dumped the grounds into the bottom, then added water to the electric kettle that sat on the counter. "Old school isn't as quick, but it tastes a helluva lot better."

"I should probably get dressed." When Eberly walked in the direction of the bedroom first, then turned toward the living room, where we'd left her sweatshirt, I caught her wrist.

"Don't." I let go of her hand, snaked my arm around her waist, pulled my shirt that hung to the middle of her thigh up, and cupped one cheek of her bare bottom. "I like you this way." I squeezed her flesh and pulled her body flush against mine. "A lot."

Eberly's breath caught, her eyes drooped closed, and she brought her hands to my shoulders when I moved her hair out of my way and kissed the soft skin beneath her ear.

As much as I didn't want to, when the kettle whistled, I let her go and poured the hot water over the coffee. Since Eberly hadn't moved, I returned to her and put my arm back around her waist. "Now, where were we?"

"You were, um…" She put her fingertips on her neck where I'd kissed her.

"You like that?"

She nodded.

"Let me hear you say it."

"I like it."

"What do you like?"

"When you kiss me."

I leaned forward and pecked her cheek. "That?"

She smiled. "Not as much."

"As what?"

"When you use your tongue."

"I see." When I kissed her in the same place I had before but trailed my mouth down the banded muscle of her neck, Eberly shuddered and pressed her body harder against mine.

After taking a deep breath, I buried my face between her shoulder and jaw. "As much as I want to continue what we're doing, there are things we need to talk about first." She stiffened in my arms and tried to wriggle away, but I tightened my hold on her waist. "I didn't say you could go anywhere."

"Trevino, I haven't…God, I can't even say it."

I brought my other hand to her face and cupped her cheek. "I think I know, and it's one of the reasons it's imperative we talk first."

"I feel so stupid," she said barely above a whisper.

"Let's start there—no more calling yourself names or referring to yourself in a disparaging way. If you do it again, there will be consequences. Do you understand?"

Her eyes blazed. "Consequences?"

"You heard me. Next, when you and I are together like this, there are certain ways I want you to address me."

Eberly's brow furrowed. "What do you mean?"

"Do you remember what you said last night when I told you to get under the covers for the *second* time?"

Other than the sweet flush of her cheeks, she didn't respond.

"Do you?"

"Yes."

"Say it again."

When she whispered, "Yes, sir," my shaft pulsed.

"When I tell you to do something, I need you to obey me."

"Obey?"

While I might've worried about her response, her hardened nipples and dilated pupils were proof enough that it excited her.

"If it's something you have a very good reason to not want to do, you can say so. It doesn't mean I'll change my mind, but I will listen. Understood?"

"Yes, sir."

"Good girl." I stroked her cheek with the pad of my thumb. "I understand that some of this may be new to you."

Eberly lowered her gaze. "Not some. All."

"Look at me." When she did, I continued. "While your physical responses convey your arousal, right now, I need to know what you're thinking. If you have concerns, I'll address them. More, if proceeding in the way I'm laying things out for you isn't something you want, this ends now. I've warned you more than once that I am not the man for you. My expectations—my demands—may be more than you can handle, but being in control is the only way I know or want to be."

"Okay."

I raised a brow. "Maybe it would be best if I gave you some time to think this over."

Eberly shook her head. "I don't need time. Except I do have a question."

"I'm sure you have many."

"Am I supposed to call you sir all the time?"

My eyes softened, and I reached down and pinched her bottom. "Right now, I'd be happy with occasionally."

"Sorry, err, sir."

"How about this? We'll work up to it. When I need it, I'll say so." I let her go and lowered the plunger to filter the coffee grounds, then got two cups from the cupboard. "How do you take it?"

"Black is fine, thanks."

I handed her the cup, then opened the refrigerator, grabbed the container of almond milk, and added some to the frother.

"Can I change my mind?"

My breath caught, and I looked over my shoulder at her. "About?"

"How I take my coffee."

I chuckled and shook my head. "You had me worried for a minute."

Eberly set the cup on the counter and rubbed her arms.

"Are you cold?"

"A bit."

"Wait for me under the blanket on the sofa. I'll bring our coffee in and light a fire."

Her eyes met mine. "Yes, sir."

When she left the room, I looked up at the ceiling. No matter how much my brain was screaming at me to end this now, my heart wasn't willing to listen. Nor was my cock. Wanting Eberly had morphed into needing her, and that wasn't something I could ignore.

8
Eberly

After snuggling under the blanket on Trevino's sofa, I rested my head against the cushion and closed my eyes. I told myself I should be freaking out, but I wasn't. Being with Trevino always calmed me. Now, even more.

The only thing that made me the least bit anxious was how turned on I was. So much so I repeatedly squeezed my legs together.

I'd hated it when Tiernan told me what to do as if he was the boss of me, but with Trevino, it felt different. Maybe it was because he said he'd listen if there was something that made me feel uncomfortable. Or maybe it was just the way he'd always treated me respectfully, even when he told me how he wanted me to address him.

Dampness flooded between my legs when I thought about the look on his face when I called him sir. I'd never felt so wanted, so desired, or so sexy.

As much as that was all I *wanted* to think about, there were other things that *needed* my attention. I'd left my cell phone in the kitchen, but the ringer was on, so if my dad did call, I'd hear it. I prayed he would soon, so I could stop worrying so much.

I also had to address the imminent foreclosure the bank threatened. "Ugh," I groaned.

"Eberly?"

I looked up and took the cup of coffee Trevino held out for me. "Sorry, and thank you."

He sat beside me. "Tell me what's on your mind."

"Where my dad has disappeared to, obviously, but how in the world are we about to lose our house? I don't understand."

He got up and lit the fireplace, then returned to the sofa. "I'll tell you as much as I know."

I turned to face him after shifting the blanket so it covered both of us. "I'd appreciate it."

"A few months ago, your father merged your winery, which basically means he sold it, to the Wine Consortium."

"He did *what*?"

Rather than repeat himself, he continued. "Shortly after he did, the consortium went public. My guess is he received shares in exchange for the winery, its inventory, and the vineyard property."

"So why are we about to lose our house?"

"Based on what Brix told me yesterday, the shares, which originally traded around ten dollars, are now worth one percent of that."

I put my head in my hands. "I can't believe this." Something occurred to me, and I looked over at him. "Is this why you covered my auction bid?"

"In part."

"You didn't need to do that. I have my own money."

"Can your father access it?"

"He cannot. In fact, that's what I heard him arguing with someone about yesterday. He told whoever he was talking to that he had no control over 'her' money. I assume now he was talking about mine." My eyes opened wide. "Wait. He *couldn't* have sold the winery."

"What makes you say that?"

"I own fifty-one percent. How could he have sold it without me knowing about it?"

"He couldn't have. Or…" Trevino's brow furrowed.

"What?"

"There are ways he could've done it fraudulently."

Fraudulently? God, this kept getting worse. As much as I didn't want to believe my dad would do something like this, how else would he have been able to sell it? "I'm going to be sick."

"Err, do you—"

"Sorry, not literally."

Trevino snuggled me close, and I rested my head on his shoulder. Being in his arms felt so good. If the shit swirling around my life would go away, I'd be happy.

"There was one other thing Brix said that I need to tell you."

"Oh my God. What else has my dad done?"

"It's about your former fiancé. My brother said he might've had something to do with your dad merging with the consortium."

I wriggled from his arms and sat up straight. "Are you fucking kidding me?"

"Do you think it's possible he could've been involved?"

I rested against the sofa and took a deep breath. "Given everything else you've told me, I wouldn't be surprised."

Trevino held out his arms. "Come back here."

"Gladly." I nestled against him and buried my face in his chest. "I'm sorry about this."

He leaned away, put his finger on my chin, and raised my head. "What do you have to be sorry for?"

"All this drama. I wouldn't blame you if you wanted to take me home right now and never see me again." From the corner of my eye, I saw his hand flex at the same time his expression darkened.

"Do you really believe I'd do that?"

"No. I mean…I don't know what I mean."

"Given everything we're talking about, I'm going to allow you one more warning. But, Eberly, the next time you disparage yourself that way, there will be consequences."

I shuddered when, instead of fear, desire made my heart pound. "What kind of consequences?"

His eyes scrunched. "I'll punish you."

"How?" I whispered.

"I haven't decided yet, but I guarantee you won't like it as much as you're thinking you will right now."

"How do you know what I'm thinking?"

"This." Trevino moved the blanket and brushed my nipple with his hand. "Your breath quickening and the way your eyes look. And if I put my hand between your legs, your pussy would be wet for me. Am I right, Eberly?"

"I'm not sure. You should—"

Before I could say another word, his hand cupped my bareness and he dragged one finger through my folds.

"Drenched."

"Trevino, God, please," I begged. I wasn't even sure what for, only that I needed something more.

"Is that the way you ask?"

I trembled under his touch. "Please, sir?"

"Good girl." He thrust one finger inside me, and I cried out. When he pressed another against my clit, I whimpered. "Should I let you come?" he asked, adding a second finger.

"Yes, sir?"

"Tell me why."

"I *need* it. No one has ever—"

His fingertips curled inside me, his thumb swirled my bundle of nerves, and pleasure like none I knew existed coursed through every part of my body. I clung to him as wave after wave of pure ecstasy radiated from between my legs. He stilled, then slowly increased the rhythm of his thrusts, deepening the pressure. "Give me one more," he demanded. "*Now*, Eberly."

"Oh, God," I groaned.

"Not God. Whose hand is bringing you such pleasure?" His fingers curled again, pressing hard against my flesh. "Say my name."

"Trevino," I cried.

"Again."

"Trevino." His name came out like a prayer the second time I said it.

"Don't ever forget that I am the man responsible for your orgasms. No one but me."

"No one but you, sir."

He shuddered, removed his hand from my pussy, and brought it to my neck. He licked his fingers, then thrust his tongue into my mouth. "Taste yourself and know that's what I do to you."

For the third time in my life, someone other than me had made me come. All it had taken was Trevino's kiss.

He held me close and stroked my hair. "Thank you for the gift of your pleasure, my beautiful dove."

I wanted to thank him instead. Tell him I hadn't given him anything; I'd only received. But I couldn't speak. I held onto him as my body returned to earth. A tear leaked from my eye, and he caught it with his lips.

"One day soon, your tears will be my gifts too."

If he as much as touched my pussy, I knew I'd come again.

I heard a cell phone ringing, but it wasn't mine.

"Dammit," Trevino muttered, easing me out of his arms. "I should get that."

"Okay," I leaned against the pillow he'd propped next to me and closed my eyes.

"Hey, Sheriff."

I bolted upright, then held my breath, waiting for Trevino to speak again. When he walked toward me, his eyes were riveted to mine.

"Yeah, send it over, and we'll take a look."

"What?" I asked when he ended the call and sat beside me.

"He said there's footage from your security camera of the guy he thinks was at your gate last night."

I gasped. "Who was it?"

"Vader's hoping you'll know."

Trevino's phone pinged, and he swiped the screen. When an image of a man appeared in the grainy video, both of us gasped.

9
Bit

One look, even as pixelated as the image was, and I knew the man who'd been at Eberly's gate was the same one I saw walk into the event center two nights ago. More concerning, though, was that she knew him too.

"Who is it?" I asked.

"Tiernan. My ex-fiancé."

"What's his last name?"

"Burke."

My mind raced with what I knew about FAIM, the Killeens, and the two men who'd attacked me—Eddie Grogan and Clint O'Donnell. I couldn't recall anyone with the surname Burke.

"Any idea what he might've wanted?" I asked.

"I wouldn't have said this earlier, but do you think he knows something about my dad?" Her face turned ashen.

"Why wouldn't he have called you?"

"I blocked his number."

"Can you unblock it?"

Eberly bit her lip. "Do you think I should try to call him?"

"Maybe. I'll let Vader, err, the sheriff, know we've been able to identify the guy, then see what he says."

"This may seem like a stupid question to ask at a time like this, but why do you call him Vader?"

I leveled my gaze at her.

"What? Wait. I meant silly. That's probably not any better. *Odd*?"

"I'll take odd. If you ever heard him over the phone, you'd know." I picked up my cell to give him an update. "Eberly's pretty sure she knows who it is. A guy named Tiernan Burke."

"Her former fiancé?" Vader asked.

"That's right. Do I want to know how you knew that?"

"Not right now, you don't," he responded.

"Gotcha."

"I'll be in touch later."

"Hang on. One more question. Should Eberly try to contact him?"

"That's a hard no."

"What did he say?" she asked when the call ended.

"He wants you to hold off on calling him."

"What about the other thing you said? About not wanting to know how he knew something."

"When I gave him the name, he knew the two of you were previously engaged."

Her eyes opened wide. "That's concerning."

"I was gonna say odd, but we'll go with your word." I winked and she half smiled. "Why don't you try your dad again?"

"Yeah. I should."

When Eberly got up and went into the kitchen, I sent two texts. The first was to a guy I'd met a few months ago. His name was Decker Ashford, and at the time, he was looking into the kidnapping of Daphne Cullen, Cru's fiancée. When I happened to come out of a bar in Paso Robles and heard her name mentioned, I'd recorded the rest of the conversation. It ultimately led to the kidnappers' arrests.

Might need some help digging up dirt on a guy, I wrote.

Decker responded right away. *Let me know what I can do.*

The next was to my brothers. *Need to call a meeting*, I wrote.

When? Bris responded.

As soon as possible.

"Any luck?" I set my phone down and asked when Eberly returned to the living room.

She shook her head. "It rings, then goes to voicemail."

"Can you think of anyone who might know where he is?"

"I called Baron Van Orr last night, but he said it had been weeks since he spoke to him. Given they've been best friends most of their lives, I found that concerning."

"Anyone else?"

"I thought about the woman who was with him at the Wicked Winemakers' Ball, but I have no idea how to contact her. I don't even know her last name."

"You know who might?"

Eberly shook her head.

"Alex." Since it was close to nine and she and her husband had a kid, I figured it wasn't too early to call.

"Hey, Bit," she answered. It used to be the one person who called me that was Cru, but in the last few months, it became more common. Admittedly, I liked it more than I used to.

"Hey, Al. Do you have a guest list for this year's ball?"

"Is that a serious question?"

"Of course it is."

"There's your answer. *Of course* I do."

"Can you tell me the name of the woman Malcolm Warwick brought with him?"

"I'll have to look that one up. Gimme a sec."

I put my finger over the phone's mic and shuddered when the lingering scent reminded me that, not very long ago, it had been inside the woman beside me. "So, uh…I forgot what I was going to say."

"Something about Alex and finding Nancy's name?"

"Right. She's looking it up."

"Here it is," said my sister. "Do you want her phone number too?"

"Definitely. Go ahead whenever you're ready."

"Nancy Burke, and her number is…" She rattled it off, and as I repeated it out loud, Eberly punched it into her phone.

"Thanks, Al, I appreciate this." I ended the call and set my phone down. "Nancy's last name is Burke."

Eberly's mouth gaped. "Get the fuck out. Seriously?"

I raised a brow and smiled at her reaction. I couldn't recall having heard her curse. "The plot thickens."

"Should I call her now?" she asked.

"Why wait? Except maybe don't let on that your dad's been gone since yesterday."

"Good thinking," she agreed.

"Put the call on speaker."

When she did, we both heard the phone ring; after two, it switched over to voicemail.

"Hey, Nancy. This is Eberly Warwick calling. I had a quick question for you if you'd please get back to me at your earliest convenience, I'd appreciate it." She left her number. Less than five minutes later, Nancy returned the call.

"Hey, thanks for responding so quickly," I began.

"Sure. What's your question?"

"I'm visiting a friend and haven't been able to reach my dad. He doesn't happen to be with you, does he?"

"No. Sorry. I haven't seen him since he dropped me off Saturday night," she responded.

"Right. My apologies for bothering you."

I held my phone to my ear and mimicked dialing.

"One last thing. Do you remember the last time you spoke to him?"

"As I said, Saturday night."

"Oh, right. Well, thanks again."

"Good job," I said when she ended the call.

"Sadly, I've gotten used to dealing with fake people."

I cocked my head.

"Let's just say that if Isabel Van Orr smells blood in the water, she'll attack like a shark." Eberly lowered her hand that held the phone and looked at me with wide eyes. "If she's telling the truth, where did my dad go after the ball? You were there when he came home the following morning."

"Good question. Is there anyone else you can think of who might've seen or talked to your father?"

Eberly shook her head.

"There are some people who might be able to help us. One is a guy who specializes in, uh, locating people.

I sent him a text earlier, and he responded asking how he can help."

Her eyes scrunched. "Why did you hesitate when you said he specializes in finding people?"

I chuckled. "That barely scratches the surface of what this guy does."

"Can you tell me his name?"

"Decker Ashford. Have you heard of him?"

"Yes, but I can't remember where or when. Does he know the Butlers?"

"Rumor is he worked for Laird. Something like that anyway."

"You said *some* people. Who besides Mr. Ashford?"

I made sure I didn't stutter this time. "My brothers."

"If they can help, that's great. But, um, can you take me home first? I want to freshen up, change my clothes, then visit the bank before it gets much later."

"Yes, but I want to check in with Vader again before we head over there."

"Sure. Of course."

When Eberly stood and went into the bathroom, I called him.

"Hey, Bit," he answered. I guess it wasn't only my family who'd taken to calling me by the nickname.

"Eberly wants to run by her house. Any issue with that?"

"Nah, my guys finished up over there a couple of hours ago."

"Was there any sign of someone on the property?"

"No, which makes me wonder about this Burke guy. Why call from the gate at that hour instead of attempting to access the property another way? It isn't like it would be tough to do."

"Maybe he thinks it's more secure than it is. Oh, and before I forget, Malcolm Warwick's date Saturday night was Nancy Burke. Says she hasn't talked to him or seen him since he dropped her off that night. Also, according to Eberly, he didn't come home after doing so. He arrived after nine the following morning."

"Did you say her last name was Burke?"

"I did, and, Vader, I plan to ask Ashford to do some digging. I thought I should let you know."

"Appreciate it. I'm interested to see what he comes up with."

I was about to mention what Eberly had told me about not knowing how her father sold the winery when she was the majority owner, but decided I should ask her before divulging that her dad might've committed fraud.

The other thing I kept to myself was that I'd also recognized the man. First, I wanted to run it by both Decker and the *caballeros*.

"All set?" I stood and asked when Eberly returned from the bathroom after I ended the call.

While she smiled, it didn't come through her eyes. Was there something bothering her that hadn't been a few minutes ago? I wouldn't ask now, but later, I'd get it out of her one way or another.

When we arrived at her house, the first thing we did was clean up the mess that was left in her father's study when I carried Eberly out of there two nights ago. There was no sign her father had returned, so when she took a shower in the en suite bath, I stayed in her bedroom and called Decker.

"Hey, Trevino. What can I do for you?"

I explained that Malcolm Warwick had left his house late yesterday afternoon and hadn't returned.

Then reiterated the part of the phone call Eberly had overheard. Next, I told him about Malcolm Warwick's financial trouble and how he'd somehow sold the winery out from under his daughter even though she was a majority owner.

"Interesting," he said under his breath.

"It gets even more so. Vader was able to pull footage of the guy who showed up at the gate that night. Turns out it was Eberly's ex-fiancé."

"That doesn't seem significant, Bit."

"I'm convinced he's got some connection to the people who attacked me in the caves."

"Tell me why."

"His eyes."

There were a few seconds of silence, and I wondered if Decker was looking into something or simply processing what I'd told him.

"Cat eyes?" he asked, confirming my first thought.

"Like Grogan's."

"What's the ex's name?"

"Tiernan Burke, and coincidentally, it's the same last name of the woman who Malcolm's been dating."

"There are no coincidences, young Avila. Haven't I taught you that much?"

"Yes, sir," I responded. While I'd never been in the military, Deck's tone was enough like that of a commander that my response was automatic.

"Anything else you want me to look into?"

"The Wine Consortium's financials as well as if Tiernan Burke is on their payroll."

"You got it. I'll be in touch when I know something. Oh, hang on. Are you getting the *caballeros* involved in this?" Ashford was one of the few outside of the organization who knew about the secret society.

"I plan to."

"The sooner, the better."

"Gotcha."

I hung up and heard the water shut off. Seeing Eberly's wet and naked body proved to be something I couldn't resist.

I snatched the towel she had in her hand as soon as I walked in the bathroom door. "Let me look at you," I said when she tried to cover herself. "Drop your arms."

She was so damn hot I momentarily considered stripping out of my clothes, carrying her to the bed, and spending the rest of the day fucking her senseless. Instead, I told her to turn around and took a good, long look at the curve of her spine and the dimples that drew my eye down to her delectable ass. Before I gave into temptation, I stepped forward and wrapped her in the plush terry cloth.

When she grabbed my hand and tucked it inside to cover her breast, I knew it would be a long, long time before I got my fill of Eberly Warwick. In fact, it might take the rest of my life.

I used the towel to dry her off and, when I knelt to do the back of her legs and her feet, couldn't resist leaning forward to nip her ass cheek.

Eberly giggled, and I stood and spun her around to face me.

"If you don't get yourself dressed in the next two minutes, it'll be hours before I'll be willing to let you put on a stitch of clothes."

When she scampered away, I called out to her. "What was that, Eberly? I couldn't hear you."

She looked over her shoulder. "Yes, sir."

10

Eberly

Rather than go in with me when I spoke to the bank manager, Trevino waited in the lobby, and I appreciated it. As he'd said, my family's finances weren't his business. If I had questions once the meeting was over, he offered his support.

My father would've insisted on handling it himself, which now caused concern. I couldn't say what Tiernan might've done, but no doubt, he'd make my problems his business whether I asked him to or not.

The banker's solution for halting foreclosure on the house was to bring the loan current. All it required was that I come up with two million dollars to do so.

"My understanding is the house was paid off years ago," I said.

"It was, but you and your father used it as collateral for a rather large loan, which he defaulted on."

"He may have, but I did no such thing," I informed him. "My name is also on the deed."

"Your signature is on the loan documents."

My eyes scrunched when he turned the papers around so I could see it. "This says it was notarized."

"Bank policy requires for it to be."

I picked the paper up to take a closer look. "Wouldn't a notary be required to sign as well?" I asked, pointing to the stamp.

He held out his hand, and I returned the document. "This is odd. That page appears to be missing. I can check the record book, but based on this date, it could've been one of two people, neither of whom still work for the bank."

"Were they fired for committing fraud?"

His expression darkened. "I'm confident every procedure was executed as required, Miss Warwick."

"And yet the notary's signature is missing."

"The page is missing, but your signature is not."

I took another look at it. It was close but not exact. "What type of identification would this have required?"

"We require it to be government issued."

Which meant, if the notary had, in fact, checked it, my father had either sneaked my driver's license from my wallet or used my passport. The latter would've been easier, given I kept it in the family safe. Still, shouldn't I have been required to be present?

"I need some time to think this over."

"If the demand isn't settled by the close of business, foreclosure will commence," he responded. "We've extended the grace period to bring the account current several times."

I had the letter I'd found on my father's desk with me and retrieved it from the envelope. It did say that it was the final notice. "I'll contact you within a couple of hours," I said, standing. "May I have a copy of the loan documents, please?"

"Of course. It will take a few minutes."

"I'm not leaving without it."

When he escorted me out of his office, I joined Trevino in the waiting area. Rather than ask about the meeting, he took my hand in his and pulled me down to sit in the chair next to him.

"I'm waiting for copies of some of the documents. Then, if you don't mind, I'd like to discuss my options with you."

Everything inside me felt like it was melting when he brought my hand to his lips and kissed my palm.

"Happy to, little dove." His phone vibrated, and he swiped the screen, looked at it for a second, then stuck it in his pocket.

"Is everything okay?"

"Yeah. I need to make a call, though."

"Go ahead. I'll wait here."

He studied me, stood, and went outside. I was so grateful for Trevino's support, and I certainly liked being with him, but how in the world had I gotten here? I leaned against the chair and folded my arms.

It was on a lark that I'd responded to a job posting for an event planner—something I had no experience doing outside of the things we'd hosted at our family's winery. That was in the middle of July, and three days later, Trevino had hired me to work for him at Los Caballeros.

Eight days ago, I was supposed to marry another man. Less than two days ago, I bid on a date with a different guy—one I would've paid twenty-five thousand dollars for if Trevino hadn't covered it for me. And a few short hours ago, I'd had the most incredible orgasm of my life brought on by a man who wanted me to call him sir and threatened to punish me if I said anything negative about myself. Somehow, I doubted that would be the only thing I'd face "consequences" for doing.

I also found out my father had sold our family business, which I was the majority owner of. That meant he'd probably forged my signature in the same way he had on the house loan that was currently in default.

Not to mention that he hadn't returned home after leaving yesterday afternoon while in the midst of what sounded like a heated argument. And despite all the times I'd called and the number of messages I'd left, he still hadn't responded. Where in the hell had he gone? Not just last night, but also after the Winemakers' Ball? The logical explanation was he was seeing another woman and he was with her. But then, why would he have brought Nancy as his date?

On top of everything going on with my dad, my former fiancé had showed up at my house late at night, repeatedly calling from the gate phone. I assumed he wanted me to let him in, but why?

I suppose it spoke volumes about the kind of life I'd led so far that it was the one time I'd felt truly afraid.

"Miss Warwick?"

"Yes," I responded, looking up at the woman who held an envelope. "Is that for me?"

"Mr. Deavers asked me to remind you that he needs a response from you before the end of the day," she said when she handed it to me.

My brow furrowed and I chuckled.

"Did I say something funny?" she asked.

"I'm not likely to forget that you're threatening to take away my home."

"Well, not me personally."

"What's your name?" I asked.

She raised her chin. "Priscilla."

There was no telling what I might have said to her had Trevino not walked in before I could respond.

"Ready?" I stood and asked.

"Hi, err…Trev," the woman said in a way that sounded far too familiar.

"Priscilla," he responded.

I looked between the two of them.

"I didn't know you were in town. It's really good to see you." When she dropped her gaze to the floor and her cheeks flushed, I spun on my heel and stalked out.

"Hey! Eberly!" Trevino shouted a few seconds later, but I kept walking.

I clutched the envelope she'd given me to my chest and shook my head. "Do not cry. Do not fucking cry," I repeated under my breath. "And do not run."

"Eberly!" I heard him call out again, but this time, he sounded as though he was getting closer, not that I'd turn around and look. Seconds later, his arm snaked around my waist. "Stop, dammit."

"Don't!" I snapped, trying to pry his hand loose.

"We aren't doing this here or now," he said, turning me in his arms.

"I don't want to do it at all."

"She isn't anything to me."

"But she used to be, and don't even think about lying to me."

He shook his head. "Stop this, Eberly."

"You know what? The last eight days have been the worst of my life since my mom died. I have a lot of shit to deal with, and as that condescending twit reminded me, I have a few hours left to make sure I don't lose my home."

"You said you wanted to talk to me about options."

"I changed my mind."

He leaned closer. "Why?"

"*Hi, err…Trev.* She was about to call you sir, wasn't she?"

He gripped my neck with one hand and tightened his other arm around my waist, bringing my body up against his. "We aren't having this conversation."

"You're right. I don't have time to lose my mind right now, so if you'll please let me go, I'd appreciate it."

"No. Not when you're this upset."

"I'm not asking, *Trev*."

He sighed and looked up at the sky. "There are things I need to tell you. Would you please just come with me?"

"I have zero interest in hearing about Priscilla or any other woman—"

When he silenced me with a kiss, I didn't bother struggling or trying to move my mouth away; I clung to him as tears streamed down my cheeks.

"It's all too much," I whispered when he released my lips but brought my head to his chest and stroked my hair.

"I know it is."

"I'm sorry."

Trevino kissed the side of my face. "Let's go." Instead of walking in the direction of the bank, Trevino took my hand and led me across the street to the town park. Thankfully, it was mostly empty at this time of day. My head was so full of noise that there wasn't room for more. "Tell me what you found out," he said after leading me to a bench, where we both sat.

"My signature was forged on the loan that's currently in default. In order to avoid foreclosure, I have to come up with two million dollars. I'm not even sure the house is worth that much."

"It is. The next question is, do you have access to that amount of money?" he asked.

"Not by the end of the day."

"May I?" he asked, motioning to the envelope. I removed the documents and handed them to him.

"The last page, where the notary would've signed, is missing."

He raised a brow, then continued skimming the pages. "Other than the page you referenced, the rest appears to be in order."

"That isn't my signature."

"Earlier, I said there are things I need to tell you." He returned the documents to me, and I put them in the envelope.

I looked off in the distance, took a deep breath, and let it out slowly. "Go ahead."

"When I stepped outside at the bank, it was to return Decker Ashford's call. I asked him to look into several things, including your former fiancé, along with the woman who was your father's date Saturday night. The other thing I asked him to do was see what he could find out about your father's sale of the winery to the consortium. And finally, what information there was about the public offering. He doesn't have an update on much of that yet, but he was able to piece together a chain of events leading to your father's current financial issues."

I turned to face him. "How bad is it?"

"Curious as much as concerning."

"In what way?"

"According to Ashford, it appears your parents went through a great deal of money in the time leading up to your mother's death."

"Neither of them ever discussed finances with me, outside of my trust, and that was set up when I was a baby."

"In his defense, I'm sure your mom's illness took a big toll on him. Then, the following year, the wine industry took a significant hit due to the global pandemic."

"I remember."

"As of eight months ago, his reserves, including investment accounts, were depleted."

I knew the time was significant, but how? "Wait. Is that when he arranged for Eberly Winery to merge with the Wine Consortium?"

"That's right," Trevino confirmed.

"Where did all the money go, though?"

"Decker's still working on tracing it."

"I don't suppose he has any idea where my dad is."

Trevino shook his head. "Also, I made arrangements for additional security, including surveillance to monitor the entirety of the estate in the event he reappears."

My eyes opened wide. "When did you do that?"

"Earlier today."

When I put my head in my hands, Trevino wrapped his arms around me.

"I wish I could rewind the clock."

"How far?" he asked.

"I'd say eight days ago, or nine, but it sounds like five years would be better. Not that I'd have any idea how to change the outcome." I put my hand on his arm. "Earlier, when I said the last few days have been the worst of my life, I didn't mean things with you."

He kissed my forehead. "I know."

"I'm grateful for your help. I don't know what I'd do without it." I sighed. "You're different than I thought you were."

Trevino raised a brow and smirked.

"I'm not talking about *that*. We didn't talk very much. Or you didn't. I've always been a chatterbox."

"Eberly, we need to talk about Priscilla."

I shook my head. "We don't."

"The time we spent together was brief as well as insignificant."

"She might not agree with the last part," I said under my breath.

"We weren't compatible, and it ended soon after it began."

I put my hand on my stomach. "Please don't tell me more."

"I won't about her, but I will about you."

I cringed. "You do remember I said that everything happening in my life is too much right now?"

"You also said I don't talk much."

"An understatement," I muttered.

"Typically, I don't bother to unless it's necessary. What I'm about to say is."

"Can we *please* not do this now?" I pleaded.

"I like you, Eberly. I have since the day I met you."

"Yeah? And when was that?"

He cocked his head. "Your interview."

"We met before, more than once, not that you noticed."

"Did we talk?"

I smirked. "I probably did. You definitely didn't."

"I'd say I'm sorry, but I'm not."

"Seriously?" My mouth gaped.

He moved his hand to my neck. "We met, or got to know each other, when we were supposed to."

"Fate, huh?"

"You don't believe in it?"

"I didn't. I'm starting to now, though." I sighed a second time. "While I'd like to forget about everything happening in my life outside of being with you, I can't.

I have until the end of the day to decide what to do about the house."

"I need to return another call."

"Should I leave?"

He smirked again. "I dare you to try." Without taking his arm from around me, Trevino pulled out his cell phone and brought it to his opposite ear.

11
Bit

"What were you able to find?" I asked when Zin, one of the *caballeros* as well as an attorney, picked up.

"I was about to send you a message. I wasn't able to locate proof that a record of an Intent to Cure was served on the Warwick property. In fact, there's no indication one was filed."

"How much time will filing one buy?"

"Fifteen days minimum. Here's the thing, Bit. I'd have to get in front of a judge in order to force the bank to do it."

"Can you make that happen today?"

"I'm working on it. Is there anything you can tell me that would compel a justice to issue the order?"

"Eberly's signature was forged on the loan documents. While there is a notary stamp, the page with his or her signature is missing."

"What about a number?"

I held out my hand, and Eberly removed the loan papers from the envelope and gave them to me. I flipped to the last page. "I didn't notice this before, but comm number is smudged."

"There should be a name printed on the stamp."

"There isn't."

"That'll do it. Along with the request for Intent to Cure, I'll also see if I can file for an emergency injunction."

"Thanks, Zin." I noticed Eberly's eyes open wide and held the phone away from my ear so she could hear the rest of what he was saying.

"You got it, Bit. By the way, you do know that Eberly is my cousin."

"Actually, I wasn't aware."

"His dad and my mom were siblings," she said when I glanced over at her.

"It would be a good idea to bring my father in on this. He'll know some of the history I don't," Zin suggested.

"I'd like that," Eberly whispered.

"Sounds good," I told him before the call ended. "So I guess you heard most of that," I said to Eberly.

"I did, and while I've never heard of an Intent to Cure, if it will buy me fifteen days, that's what matters."

"I had no idea you and Zin were related."

"To be honest, I know his dad better than I do him. He's my godfather. Uncle Michael is also the trustee for the money my mother left me."

I made a mental note to call my uncle, Tryst. He, Michael Oliver, and Malcolm Warwick were active members of Los Caballeros at the same time my dad was. It would be interesting to hear his take on Eberly's father's actions.

For now, though, my little dove needed my undivided attention. While I hadn't set ground rules with her in the way I would've in another relationship like the one I intended she and I have, I needed to. I couldn't punish her now when I hadn't made my expectations—and the subsequent consequences—clear.

"Let's go home. There are a few things I need to take care of."

Her eyes darted between mine. "Home?"

"For the foreseeable future, until we can make sure your house and the grounds are more secure, that means the cottage. Are you good with that?"

I saw the glimmer of a smile, which she quickly masked. "That depends on what things you need to take care of."

"I misspoke. Not a thing, little dove. You."

"Then, yes, I'd like to go home."

Once in my truck, I buckled Eberly in, then rested my right hand on her thigh. "I like you better in dresses." I walked my fingers up closer to her core, then cupped her mound. "And no panties."

"The weather's kind of chilly for that."

"Move your hair out of my way." I leaned over and kissed the side of her neck. "What I have planned will keep you warm."

Eberly shuddered.

"First, though, there's the matter of you taking off on me and not stopping when I told you to."

Her eyes opened wide. "But…"

"Say it."

"I was angry."

"Is that an excuse to treat me disrespectfully? Was I disrespectful to you?"

"No."

"Would you agree there should be consequences for your behavior?"

"Um, I guess so."

"How about this? If you do what I ask between here and the cottage, I'll let the earlier behavior go."

She studied me. "Okay."

I put the truck in gear, backed out of the bank's parking lot, and got on the road. "Unfasten your jeans."

"What did you say?"

"You heard me."

Her hands shook as she released the button and lowered the zipper.

"Move them and your panties down to your knees."

She hesitated, but then lifted her bottom.

"I didn't hear your response."

Her head jerked in my direction. "Yes, sir?"

"That's better."

When she did as I asked, I could immediately smell her arousal. I caught her wrist and brought her hand to my lips, capturing her index and middle finger in my mouth. "Now, touch yourself," I said, releasing her arm. "Eberly?" I added when she didn't respond.

"Yes, sir."

We were at a stoplight, but with as high as my truck was lifted, anyone other than a semi driver wouldn't be able to see when she eased both digits between her folds. I grabbed her wrist a second time and brought her fingers to my mouth again. When the light changed, I released her hand. "I didn't tell you to stop."

Her eyes were hooded and her nipples rock hard when she stuck those fingers between her legs.

I was about to pull through the gates of Los Caballeros and said, "If you make yourself come by the time we reach the cottage, we'll forget about your earlier disrespectful behavior."

"But…"

"Say it, Eberly."

"I want *you*, sir. I need you."

I stopped short of my usual parking spot and took the truck out of gear. "Make yourself come now, and you'll have me." My eyes bored into hers. "Do it."

She grabbed my arm with her free hand, and her fingernails dug into my flesh. With my opposite hand, I caught her nipple between two fingers and squeezed.

"Oh, God," she groaned, and her breath caught.

"That's it. Give it to me, little dove."

She held tight as the orgasm rocked her body. When her breathing evened out, I put the truck in gear and drove the short distance to the cottage.

"You can pull them up but do not fasten your jeans. As soon as we're inside, I want you to strip out of your clothes and wait for me in the living room."

"Yes, sir." Her voice was deep and breathy. In the next couple of hours, I planned to make her scream my name in pleasure so many times that she wouldn't be able to even talk tomorrow.

I was about to follow her into the house when my phone rang. When I saw it was Zin, I accepted the call.

"I'll be in front of the judge at three this afternoon," he began. "My prediction is I'll be successful in getting the Intent to Cure, which means Eberly or her father will still have to bring the loan current; it'll just give them more time. If we're able to get an injunction, it will mean there'll be time to prove the loan was approved fraudulently. Which is a whole other can of worms. I need to know how Eberly wants to proceed if it comes to that, given it's her father who defrauded her."

"Understood."

"To be clear, though, an injunction, or even her dad being prosecuted, doesn't mean either of them will be off the hook for the money. The bank isn't going to let two million dollars go without a fight—unless, of course, they were a party to the fraud."

"What do you need from Eberly and me?"

"First, I need her to hire me so I can prove I'm the attorney of record. Second, the judge may want to hear from her. Best if you meet my dad and me at my office no later than two. Half past one would be better if you can make it happen."

I checked the time. While it gave us close to two hours, it was nowhere near enough for what I had planned.

"Understood, and we'll be there."

The call ended, and I went inside to find a naked Eberly waiting for me. Good God, I wanted to sink my cock into her pussy, but it would have to wait. There was no way I'd rush her giving me the precious gift of her virginity.

I walked over to her on the sofa, spread my legs, then pulled her between them. "Get on your knees for me, little dove."

I held out my hands, and she took them to steady herself. Once she was in front of me, I tightened my grip.

"When you were on your way inside, I received a call from Zin. He was able to schedule time in front of a judge this afternoon. Also, his father will be joining us. That's if you want me to go with you."

Eberly squeezed my hands. "Of course I do."

"What this means is we'll need to put our plans for the afternoon on hold."

"Oh."

"However, since you were such a good girl for me on our way home, I think you deserve a reward."

She caught her lip in an effort not to smile, but I saw it anyway.

"Come on, on your feet. I'm hungry."

"That's my reward? You're going to feed me?"

I raised a brow.

"Sir?"

"I didn't say anything about you eating."

"Should I get dressed, s-s-sir?"

"No." I held her hand and led her into the kitchen and over to the island. I put my hands on her waist and lifted her so her bottom rested on it. "Lie back for me." I eased her down on the cold granite, then spread her legs.

"I'm, um…" she stammered.

I put my hands on the top of her thighs. "Go ahead. You're what?"

"Uncomfortable."

I grinned. "Would a pillow help?"

Eberly shook her head. "That isn't what I mean."

"Are you telling me you don't want me to eat? But I'm starving."

She smiled and rolled her eyes. "Very funny."

My brow furrowed. "There will come a time when you will not get away with all you have, Eberly. But until we've had a chance to talk about my expectations, I'll let things like you rolling your eyes at me go. I'm also asking you to trust that, right now, I know what you need."

"Okay."

I raised a brow. "You're pushing it, little dove."

"Yes, sir."

When I spread her pussy, leaned down, and blew on her clit, Eberly's spine arched. When I licked through her folds, she whimpered, and when I used my tongue and fingers, she screamed my name before her essence flooded my mouth. I made her come twice more, then gathered her in my arms, carried her into the bedroom, and held her close to me.

It was all I could do not to fuck her. My cock strained against the zipper of my jeans to the point it was painful, but this wasn't about my pleasure. I planned to make the first time she felt me inside her so mind-blowing that no other man could ever satisfy her.

While Eberly showered, I called Snapper to see how the beefed-up version of security was coming along at Eberly Winery.

"Hey, Bit. I was about to call you," he said like Zin had. "There's some shit goin' on over here I figured Eberly would want to know about."

"What specifically?"

"There's a crew moving inventory out. Another truck arrived a few minutes ago, and it looks like they're about to load equipment."

"Fuck," I said under my breath. "Any sign of Malcolm?"

"Negative. What do you want me to do?"

"I'll contact Zin. He's arranged to get in front of a judge to delay the foreclosure on the house. If he can convince him there's a case to be made for the winery being sold fraudulently as well, we may be able to get another injunction to prevent the removal of property. In the meantime, get in touch with Vader and let him know what we've got in the works. I'll call you back as soon as I finish running this by Zin."

"Who were you talking to?" Eberly asked when she came out of the bathroom.

"Snapper. He said there are people removing inventory from your winery. So far, no sign of your dad, though."

Her eyes opened wide.

"You probably heard me say I was about to call Zin."

When she came over and sat on a stool near the kitchen island, all I could picture was how she'd looked with her legs spread for me.

"Excuse me for a sec," I said, stepping into the living room to place the call, not that it helped wipe the image from my mind.

"We've got another issue," I began when Zin answered. After I explained what Snapper had reported was happening at the winery, he said he'd contact

Vader directly and ask him to send deputies to stop the removal of assets until this afternoon's hearing.

"Can he do that?"

"As sheriff, it's within his power. Given what we know so far, I think he'll agree to in order to buy us some time."

I thanked him and returned to the kitchen, where Eberly waited.

"Zin's on it, but now, I should give Snapper an update."

"Do you want me to leave?"

I stepped closer, stood behind her, and wrapped one arm around her waist. "From now on, whenever I'm in this kitchen, I'm going to picture you lying on this island naked, little dove. I went into the other room so I could focus on the call I had to make, not to hide anything from you. Understood?"

"Yes, err, sir."

"Unless we're in the middle of what is referred to as a scene, you do not have to call me sir. In fact, it's best if you don't since every time you do, I'll be distracted by what I plan to do to you next."

Eberly leaned against me. "I'm thinking about that too."

I moved her hair and kissed her neck. "It's taking every ounce of control I have to remain focused on the issues with your house and the winery. But after we've met with Zin and the judge, all of my attention will be on you."

"When do we have to leave?"

"In about an hour."

"I'd like to walk over to the Stonehouse and do a quick check on the gardens."

There was no reason for me to think Eberly would be in danger while on the Los Cab estate, except the thought of not being with her made me anxious, particularly since, at the time of my attack, the property should've been impenetrable too. "I'll go with you."

"I swear this is one of the most beautiful places on earth," Eberly said as we walked along the trail that led to the old winery.

"Since I grew up here, I take it for granted. There are a couple of other places I feel that way about."

"Yeah? Where?" she asked.

"My uncle has a place in Mexico. He calls it *El Lugar de Curación*, which translates to the healing place."

"How beautiful. What made him give it that name?"

"His wife Rosa was very sick," I began, wishing I hadn't brought it up. Like Tryst's late wife, Eberly's mom lost her battle to cancer. "He'd hoped the ranch's magic would cure her."

I glanced at Eberly, who was looking down at the ground.

"Sorry," I muttered.

"Don't be. I'd love to hear more about it."

"The story Tryst tells is that when he was in the military, he and his unit were stationed in Mexico. He went for a walk on his own and got lost. When he walked up a ridge to try to get his bearings, Rosa was there too. She and her family were visiting the area. Anyway, he's always said that, in his very first conversation with her, he promised to one day buy land in the valley below where they stood and build a home for her."

"How romantic."

I chuckled. "I have a hard time believing that's what really happened."

She shook her head, but she was smiling. "Cynic."

"I suppose I am. On the other hand, when I recall visits there when I was younger, I remember experiencing a sense of peace like nowhere else on earth."

"Wow. That's quite a statement."

"My uncle is a follower of Hinduism. There's a certain style of architecture, called vastu shastra, which relates to it. He used it for all the buildings on the ranch. Even Brix's house here, which is actually Cru's now."

"I'm not familiar with it, but it sounds intriguing."

"It's been a while since I visited, but the last time I was there, he'd recently rebuilt a meditation center after a fire burned the previous one to the ground. There's also a chapel, a main house, and several guest casitas. Oh, and a therapeutic riding center."

"It sounds amazing. I'd love to see it one day."

"It really is, and you should." I didn't go as far as telling Eberly I wanted to take her there or that I thought a visit to the place might help ease the tension she was experiencing over things with her father.

I stopped walking when something occurred to me. Could the ranch be where Malcolm Warwick had disappeared to? If he had, wouldn't Tryst have said so by now? As soon as I had the chance, I'd call him and ask outright.

12

Eberly

Since I called Trevino in the middle of the night and he brought me to Los Cab, he and I hadn't been apart longer than the length of a shower. On one hand, I liked it. Until I knew what was going on with my dad, I was skittish. On the other hand, the more attached I got to him, the harder it would be once everything was sorted and things returned to the way they originally were. Because they would, wouldn't they?

Like Tiernan, I didn't doubt Trevino would eventually find me lacking, given my innocence and inexperience, and he'd either move on or return to women like Priscilla who probably knew when to call him sir and when not to.

While I'd always been introverted, even shy, I had moments of sticking up for myself. Even times when I was emboldened. Sadly, those were fewer and farther between before I turned into a metaphorical doormat.

Was that why my father had thought nothing of forging my name on legal documents where he'd basically cheated me out of a business I was part owner of? Not to mention—our house? I couldn't imagine how he thought I'd react. Did he think I'd just go along with it without question? And what now? Fraud was a crime. Was he counting on me looking the other way, not wanting him to be in trouble for it?

Admittedly, a part of me didn't. I wasn't certain, but maybe he could even go to jail for what he'd done.

The other thing bothering me was I knew my parents had significant wealth. What had happened to all that money?

And what about his relationship with Tiernan? Were my dad and him in cahoots the entire time? Had he decided not to marry me because he realized my father had no money left? Or was it because my dad had told him he had no control over or access to my trust fund? Or was it simply because he thought I was boring?

I clenched my fists at my sides. The farther I walked, the more I hated how *unworldly* I was. Not that I had any idea how to become more so. Not in life in general, and particularly not in relationships. Specifically—sex. Trevino was the first man who'd opened that door for me, and barely so far.

The very things I couldn't stand about Tiernan, like the way he'd tried to control me, were, at least in part, similar to how Trevino treated me. Except it *felt* so different. No, it *was* so different. He respected me. I didn't know that from his words alone; I knew it from his actions.

God, when he'd told me to unfasten my jeans and touch myself, I almost had an orgasm from his words alone. Would that grow tiresome for him? Would he lose interest once he realized I wasn't just inexperienced, but also unimaginative? What then? Would he decide we weren't compatible and end things shortly after they began? That was what he said had happened with *Priscilla*.

"Eberly?" I heard him say from a few paces behind me when I reached the gate leading into the Stonehouse gardens.

I spun around on him but couldn't speak. My nerves were frayed, and my emotions were in a state of chaos. Nothing good would come of me sharing my thoughts right now.

He got closer, but I took a step away.

"Hey, what happened between the time we left the cottage and now?"

I folded my arms, and my eyes filled with tears. "I can't tell you."

His brow furrowed. "Why not?"

I looked up at the sky. "Because I'm *feeling* really stupid right now. I know you told me not to say things like that about myself, but I can't help how I feel. And if you don't want to hear it, you shouldn't ask."

"Can I touch you?"

"Yes."

He took two more steps and put his hands on my shoulders. "I remember the first day we worked together. We were in this very spot, and you shared your ideas for the old winery with me."

"That isn't helping," I muttered.

"What do you mean?"

"I already said I was feeling stupid. I know I overstepped that day."

He shook his head. "What you did was dazzle me, both with your exuberance and your vision. Then, when we went inside, rather than seeing a filthy, dilapidated space, you told me to picture a couple dancing."

My cheeks flushed with embarrassment, and he stroked my face with his fingertips.

"When Alex announced the details of the date I offered in the bachelor auction, it didn't dawn on you that what I planned was in an effort to recreate our time together that afternoon?"

"It might have."

He smiled. "Can you say—honestly—that you didn't realize how often I invented ridiculous reasons to stop by here when I knew you'd be working? That the reason I did was so I could see you?"

"I thought I was imagining it because I wanted it so badly."

Trevino leaned down and kissed me, then stroked my hair. "I can't stop you from feeling regret about the things that are happening with your father, but none of it is your fault or your doing."

"That wasn't what I was thinking about."

"Will you share with me what it was?"

I gulped and took a deep breath. "I'm *inexperienced*."

"And you think I don't like it?"

"Maybe you do now, but what if you get, you know, bored?"

"I worry more that the way I am will be too much for you."

"I like it," I whispered.

"Little dove, we have barely scratched the surface of how I am, what I need." An alarm went off on his phone. "Dammit, I'm sorry, but we need to leave."

I dropped the arms I'd put around him, but he put them back.

"Later, we'll talk about the things we should have already. For now, we need to make sure your house, and maybe even the winery, is protected. Okay?"

He kissed me again when I said it was.

"Know this. I won't get bored, Eberly."

"How can you be sure?"

He rested his forehead against mine. "I'll tell you later."

When we walked into Zin's law office, Uncle Michael met us as we walked in the door. He held his arms out to me, and as I fell into his embrace, I thought about how much I needed this from my own father. He could be demonstrative, but it wasn't that often. Not like my mom had been. Tears ran down my cheeks as I thought about how much I missed her but also how good it felt to have her brother comfort me.

"Thank you for being here," I said, wiping my tears.

"We'll get this sorted," he said, motioning me into the conference room before shaking Trevino's hand. "Thank you for all you're doing," I heard him say.

Zin pulled out a chair for me and waited until Trevino was seated beside me before he and his father took seats themselves.

"Before we go any further, there's something I need to ask you, Eberly. You may not be able to answer me right away, and that's fine, but it's something you need to think about," said my uncle.

"How to handle what my dad's done?"

"That's right. We don't know the whole story, so most of what we're going on are the facts as they've presented themselves. There is a chance that if everything is as it looks, your father may face legal ramifications."

"I've considered he might."

"Have you come to any conclusions?"

Trevino reached over and took my hand.

"I want to hear his side of the story, but at the same time, I can't lose the house because of it." No one understood why not more than my uncle. It was where he and my mother grew up. When my parents married, they moved into a guesthouse on the property, and when my grandmother passed away, my granddad took the smaller house. He insisted my parents live in the bigger one, and while I wasn't born yet, my mom was pregnant with me at the time.

"It wasn't his to use as collateral," I said, looking into Uncle Michael's eyes. "He knew I wouldn't agree to it, which is why he handled it the way he did."

"It's easy to make that assumption," said Zin. "However, we need to give him the same benefit of the doubt the court would."

"I agree," I responded.

"I think what my dad is saying is, if it comes down to it and your father is facing prosecution, you will need to decide whether you want to press charges. The decision may also be taken out of your hands. The main thing is that you're aware of the possibility."

"I am."

Trevino squeezed my hand when I glanced over at him. I hoped he knew how much I appreciated him being here and, for the second time, not interjecting his opinion.

"One thing we'll be asking for this afternoon is to subpoena the sales documents for Eberly Winery. I believe, given the questionable nature of the loan documents, the judge will grant the order," said my uncle.

As much as I didn't want confirmation that my father had done the same thing with the sale of the winery as he did with the house, I had to know. If there was any way for me to save it, I couldn't stop short.

I couldn't believe it, but by the end of the hearing, the judge had granted everything Zin asked for. In addition to the injunction preventing the foreclosure on the house, there was an order stopping the removal of any assets from the winery.

Now, it was imperative we find my dad. There was a good chance he'd disappeared intentionally, not knowing how to handle telling me we'd lost everything. What I had no idea how to do was get in touch with him to tell him what I needed more than anything was for him to come home.

When we returned to Zin's office and I said as much, Trevino asked to speak with me privately.

"I have an idea, Eberly, but I can't share exactly what it is with you yet. I'm asking you to trust me on this."

I stared into his eyes. "I do," I said without hesitation.

He brought my hand to his lips and kissed my palm. "I can't tell you what that means to me. How much I'm honored by it."

I sensed there was more he had to say, and whatever it was, I wouldn't like. "But?"

He smiled. "It means I'll need to be elsewhere for at least a couple of hours. In turn, that means our talk will be delayed."

I hated that being apart from him for that long worried me as much as it did. A week ago, I was alone most of the time.

"I'm going to request your uncle to stay with you. Will you agree to it?" he asked as if he'd read my mind.

"Of course. I mean, if he doesn't mind."

"He will not."

13
Bit

For the second time in my short tenure, I requested an emergency meeting of Los Caballeros members, both current and the *viejos*. The two exceptions were Malcolm Warrick, for obvious reasons, and Michael Oliver, who'd agreed to stay with Eberly.

Zin had agreed to give the legal rundown of her father's recent actions while I supplied the chain of events Decker Ashford had pieced together.

Brix, who was the eldest member of the current group, led the meeting once those expected arrived. He prefaced it by saying Warwick had been "missing" for thirty-six hours, and that while Vader had begun his own investigation, he'd encouraged the *caballeros*—as well as Decker Ashford—to start their own. Given everyone in the room knew Vader well, it came as no surprise that his suggestion was off the record.

Next, Zin reviewed this afternoon's legal proceedings, which were met with stunned looks on most of the faces in the room. I hoped what I had to share would mitigate some of it.

"Go ahead, Bit," said Brix when Zin was finished.

I stood and handed out a printed timeline based on Decker's estimates.

"As you can see, Malcolm Warwick's financial troubles began in the months before his wife, Belinda, passed away. That her death was so closely followed by a global pandemic created what I believe is the perfect storm of what led to his taking out a loan on their home as well as merging Eberly Winery with the Wine Consortium."

I gave everyone the chance to look over the handout.

"May I?" Tryst asked.

"Of course."

He stood. "There is a logical assumption that can be made based on my own experience," he began. I watched as he met Baron Van Orr's gaze. I realized he too would understand. "I believe my nephew means to suggest that Belinda's terminal illness may explain the significant cash outlays in the months before she died. As I can attest, experimental cancer treatment can be quite costly and is rarely covered by insurance."

Those in the room murmured their agreement.

Tryst turned to me, then took his seat.

"The same thing occurred to me," I said. "Given most of you have known Malcolm for years, there's little else that makes sense. There were more murmurs and head nods. "The urgency, now, is finding him, and that is the reason for the emergency meeting. I'll begin by asking if anyone in the room knows where he is?"

Instead of nodding, everyone shook their heads or murmured their negative response.

Brix suggested forming teams made up of current and past members to brainstorm where he might have gone. "Bit, if you want to take off, I can give you an update once we have the first steps nailed down."

I shook my head. "Before I leave, there's something else I want to address."

"Go ahead," prompted my brother.

I cleared my throat. "Anyone who was in attendance at this year's Wicked Winemakers' Ball knows that I left suddenly and inexplicably." There were a few chuckles. "During the auction, I saw a man come in the side door, not far from the stage, where I stood. He scanned the room, and when our eyes met, I was sure he was the man who'd tried to kill me in these very caves last year. Subsequently, I learned it wasn't the same person. However, they share a unique physical trait that makes me think they're related. Their eyes."

Snapper stood, and when I signaled for him to go ahead, he spoke. "I checked, and Eddie Grogan is still in prison. However, as Bit pointed out to me, less than five percent of the world's population has amber-colored eyes."

"The man I saw Saturday night has been identified as Tiernan Burke, Eberly Warwick's former fiancé," I added. "Ashford is looking for a connection between him and Grogan as well as between him and either FAIM or the Killeens."

"Someone who obviously wasn't arrested in the FBI raid last year," said Brix.

"That's right," Snapper responded. "One possibility is he may have been in prison on other charges at the time. I'll research that angle."

"Since Vader caught him on surveillance footage, I'm assuming he was also able to see the vehicle," said my youngest brother, Rascon, who everyone called Kick.

"I believe so," Snapper responded.

"So we should be able to track him."

"We are," said Brix. "At least the vehicle he was in that night."

I raised my head. How did he know this when I didn't?

"So far, it appears he's lying low or using a different vehicle. Ashford has his team monitoring video surveillance for both vehicle and man," Brix added.

I wouldn't waste time now, but when I was able to speak with Brix alone, I'd ask why I hadn't been made aware of any of what he'd just said.

From the corner of my eye, I saw Tryst motioning to me. When I acknowledged him, he stood.

"What you're suggesting is this man may have ties to the Irish mafia as well as something to do with Malcolm's disappearance and the fraud he's allegedly committed?" he asked.

Zin spoke up. "We're speculating, but, for now, any theories we come up with are worth pursuing."

Tryst murmured his agreement.

"Unless anyone else has something to add, I believe that's it for now," I said after thanking everyone for showing up on such short notice.

Brix and Tryst walked me out.

"You wanna explain what went on in there?" I asked Brix.

"You and I both received an update from Decker during the meeting. Since you were leading it, I was able to review it first."

His response left me feeling like an asshole for confronting him, except not enough to apologize. He could've led with that information before he responded to Snapper and Kick. "How is Eberly?" my uncle asked.

"Worried, as you'd expect she'd be."

He put his hand on my shoulder and squeezed. "I have known Malcolm since we were younger than you are now. He is a good man and a better friend. While his actions may seem unfathomable, I am proud of you for presenting Decker's timeline with such grace."

"Thank you, Uncle."

My siblings and I were each close to our father's brother in our own way. We all confided in him, turned to him for advice, and accepted the comfort few could offer in the way he did. There was no one in my life I was closer to. Tryst knew about my struggles both before and after I was attacked. He also knew about the control I had to maintain in order to stave off the depression and anxiety I was so often plagued with.

His validation always meant the world to me but especially when my self-doubt and insecurity were more acute.

After I embraced him, Brix stepped forward. "I owe you an apology," he said.

"Yeah? What for?"

"Being an asshole for the last thirty-three years."

I chuckled. "You've got seven years on me, brother. I doubt you were any better before I was born."

He laughed too. "You're probably right."

"If you'll both excuse me," said Tryst, motioning in the direction of the room we'd come out of.

"Of course," I responded.

"Look, I want to say you've really impressed me these last few weeks, but it sounds condescending as hell," said Brix.

"You're right. It does."

"I have a lot of respect for you, Bit, and I'm sorry I haven't been good about saying so."

I raised a brow. "That sounds more like your wife talking than you."

He laughed a second time. "While Addison is definitely a good influence on me, I promise that this time, my words are my own."

"I appreciate it."

He returned to the room like Tryst had, and I began the slow walk out of the wine caves. With each step that took me closer to where two men had ambushed me and left me for dead, my legs and feet became heavier, as though I wore weights around my ankles that became increasingly harder to bear.

"Hey, Bit," I heard my brother Cru call from behind me. I knew his intent and was relieved to not have to walk the rest of the way alone. I stopped where I was and waited for him. Rather than put his hand on my shoulder like Tryst had, Cru walked beside me.

"There's something I want to ask you," he said when we were within a foot of the entrance to the room where the attack took place.

"Go ahead."

"I was wondering if you'd consider being my best man."

When we stepped outside the cave's entrance, I turned to face him. "Are you sure?" I asked.

"There's no one I want standing by my side more than you, brother."

"I'm honored." When he held out his hand to shake mine, I pulled him into an embrace instead. "Thank you, Enzo."

He patted my back. "Thank you, Trevino."

As I walked to my truck, I noticed his parked beside mine. "You heading home?" I asked.

"I can't stay away. I missed Daphne so fucking much."

His eyes met mine, and for the first time in my life, I understood how he felt. I ached being away from Eberly even for the length of the brief meeting. She said she feared I'd get bored with her. I was far more worried she'd get sick of me. I smiled. "I get it."

14
Bit

When I walked into the cottage, Eberly and Michael were sitting in front of the fireplace in the living room. Each held a glass of wine and was laughing.

"Don't let me interrupt," I said, walking over to kiss Eberly's cheek.

"Uncle Michael was telling stories about my mom and dad." Her eyes met mine. "Good ones."

I looked over at him and mouthed my thanks. It was exactly what she needed to offset the constant worry and suspicion she felt for the man who'd raised her. I couldn't imagine how I'd react if I believed one of my siblings was capable of the things Malcolm had done to her. It would devastate me.

"Be right back," I said, walking into the kitchen to see if there was any wine left in whatever bottle they'd opened. When I heard his footfalls, I realized Michael had followed me.

"I'm heading over to the caves now unless there's anything you want to share with me."

I shook my head. "Brix can fill you in on what we discussed."

"Eberly is fortunate to have you by her side through this, Trevino. Evelyn and I would be happy to have her stay with us, but I think she's more comfortable here with you."

"If she did stay with you, you'd have to put up with me too."

He chuckled. "I had a feeling that's what you'd say."

After pouring my wine, he and I returned to the living room and he told Eberly he'd talk to her in the morning.

I sat beside her, took her glass, and set it next to mine on the table, then put my arm around her. She snuggled closer to me and put her head on my shoulder.

"There's something I've been thinking about."

Eberly raised her head. "What's that?"

"Do you know if your mother had any experimental treatment for her illness?"

Her eyes scrunched. "She did. Oh my God, do you think that's where the money went?"

"There's a good chance. At least in part."

She put her hand on her stomach. "I should've thought of it instead of assuming the worst about my dad."

"It doesn't change some of the things he's done subsequently."

"You're right." Eberly covered her mouth when she yawned and returned her head to my shoulder.

"Come on. Let's get some sleep." I took her hand in mine.

"I thought we were going to talk."

"Not tonight."

"But—"

"I don't have the energy for it, and I know you don't either."

Her brow was furrowed.

"Are you planning on leaving anytime soon?" I asked.

"Meaning?"

"Your uncle mentioned you might want to stay with him and your aunt."

"Is that what you want?"

I leveled my gaze at her. "Answer my question, little dove."

"I'd rather stay with you unless—"

I kissed her, then pulled away. "The point I'm trying to make is I want you here with me, and as long as you're not planning to leave, then whether we talk tonight or tomorrow won't matter."

She lowered her head and frowned. "You're right."

Rather than pull her up with me when I stood, I put my arm under her and lifted her in my arms. I carried her into the bedroom, rested her on the mattress, then knelt in front of her.

"We both *want*, Eberly. I'm sure my desire for you far exceeds yours for me."

She shook her head. "I don't think that's possible."

I smiled, then leaned forward and kissed her. "I assure you, it is."

"Then, why…?"

"You know the answer, but I'll say it anyway. The first time you and I make love, I don't believe either of us wants to feel rushed or tired, or that we might be interrupted at any minute. Don't you think it's worth waiting for?"

"As long as that's the real reason."

"Are you accusing me of lying to you?"

"No. That isn't what I meant."

I stood and pulled her up with me. "I'm going to remove your clothes now. Then we'll talk."

"Now?"

"Talk, Eberly."

"Then, why are you removing my clothes?"

"That will become clear once our negotiation begins."

When her eyes widened and her breath caught, I expected more questions, but she remained silent.

I began by lifting her sweater over her head, then reaching behind to unfasten her bra. "Keep still, little dove," I said when she went to remove it from her arms.

Next, I unfastened her jeans, then stood to ease her torso down on the mattress. Kneeling again, I removed her shoes and socks, then pulled her jeans and panties from her body.

"Give me your hands." When she did, I helped her sit up and spread her legs so I could kneel between them. Apart from when my fingers brushed her skin when I removed her clothes, I hadn't touched her until I rested my hands above her knees.

"Earlier, I mentioned something called a scene. Do you remember?"

"Yes, sir."

"Good girl." I reached forward and cupped her cheek. "The reason you are naked and I am not is to establish a power-exchange dynamic between us. You, as the submissive, are bare and open for my use. By keeping my clothes on, I'm reinforcing my dominance over you as it relates to what we're about to do. In this case, we're going to talk."

Her lower lip came out, and I brushed it with the pad of my thumb.

"The best way I can explain a scene is to describe it as a defined sexual interaction with a starting and stopping point. While we are in the midst of one, I will expect you to do several things." I met her gaze and waited for her response.

It took her mere seconds to give me the "yes, sir" I wanted.

"First, you will refer to me as you just have, answering my requests and demands in a way that I know you've understood the expectation."

"Yes, sir," she repeated.

"Before anything further happens between us, we need to establish some ground rules. I alluded to those when I said you'll face consequences for your behavior."

I waited until she responded to continue.

"There will be more rules we agree upon that are based on what you determine to be your limits. For example, you may say you're uncomfortable when I ask you to make yourself come while we're in my truck, driving in places where there's a chance someone might see you."

I eased my hands up her legs and she shuddered.

"On the other hand, I think you liked that."

"I did, sir."

"However, if I asked you to do the same thing in a restaurant, you might not like it as much."

"Not at all."

I cleared my throat, and she quickly added the honorific I required. "That would be a limit. You are willing to make yourself come within the confines of a vehicle, but wouldn't want to do it in a more public place."

"I understand, sir."

"To make things easier for us both, I have a contract, if you will, that lists things you definitely want to try, things you might want to try, and others that you absolutely would not want to participate in. I will complete the same questionnaire, and we will review them together. Anything you'd like to say thus far?"

"I don't think so, sir."

"Good girl. You're doing so well."

I eased my hands up another inch.

"While it may seem as though I'm asking you to give up control when I say I want you to obey me, what is actually happening is that, by doing so, you are giving me the gift of your submission. You have the power to stop any scene that makes you uncomfortable. Know this, though. I will push you, Eberly. I will bring you to heights of pleasure like nothing you've ever known, but in order to do that, you need to *give* me that power. Do you understand?"

"I think so, sir."

"Let's talk about how you let me know where your comfort level is. Some people in this type of relationship use red, yellow, and green to communicate how they're feeling. Red would mean you want to end the scene immediately. Yellow would mean you need a minute to decide whether you'd like to continue or even take a brief break if you're overwhelmed. Green would mean you're in a good headspace and we can proceed. The alternative to using colors would be for you to pick what's known as a safe word. Once you've used it, I would stop the scene immediately and we would not continue."

"Red is fine, sir."

"Eberly, I want to be clear that if you say no, I will not stop whatever I'm doing. If you say red, I will."

"I understand."

She'd been so good to this point that I let the slip of not responding properly slide.

"Next, we'll talk about punishment. When we review the contract that includes our hard and soft limits, we will also go over my expectations in greater detail. Failure to meet them may result in consequences."

"Like what, sir?"

"As with our limits, we will discuss which forms of punishment you're willing to experience and which you're not."

"Can you give me an example?" she asked. "Err, sir?"

I smiled and kissed the tip of her nose. "Well done, little dove. And yes, one example would be I would spank you. Another might be that I don't permit you to have an orgasm."

Her eyes opened wide. "For how long?"

"That would be dependent on the behavior that warranted the consequence."

"I'll know, though, right? What you want me to do or not do?"

"You will. Typically, in no uncertain terms."

"And if I don't like something, I can use the safe word?"

"Yes, little dove, but I caution you to use them judiciously. If you say 'red,' the scene will end."

"Understood, err, sir."

"The goal, Eberly, is for you and I to experience pleasure together. It isn't about me commanding you to do things. It's about you allowing me to and accepting that, at a given moment, I know what's best or what will take you higher than you ever could've imagined.

"A perfect example of how that might occur outside of a scene is what happened this morning when you walked out of the bank in anger."

She bit her pouted lip and lowered her gaze. "I'm sorry."

"I knew then that you were. However, that is something I would consider deserving of punishment. I respectfully asked you to stop and wait for me more than once, and I asked you to explain how you were feeling. You refused to do either."

"I know. I was—"

"You said you were angry, but do you want to know what I think?"

Her eyes opened wide again. "Uh, sure…sir."

"I believe that, more than anger, what you were experiencing was a lack of control. My interaction with Priscilla left you feeling insecure, and you acted out based on your discomfort."

"I did."

"I'd like to suggest you consider that, had you waited until we left the bank together, I would've acknowledged those feelings and respectfully explained my own. I would've reassured you that the only smile I want to see throughout the day is yours." I reached up and covered her breast with one hand. "The only person I want in my bed—in my life—is you."

I put my arms on either side of her and leaned forward. "I'm crazy about you, little dove. While I know I'll never get enough of your naked body next to mine, there's so much more. You dazzle me. You also challenge me, which you may think I don't like, but I do."

"You mean when I got mad at you in my kitchen?"

"You have no idea how much that excited me. If your father hadn't arrived home when he did, there's no telling what I might've done." I sighed. "There's one more thing I need to say, and this might be the most important of all."

"I'm listening."

"When I'm with you, I feel safe. Not judged or discounted—you accept me as I am, who I am, and how I am. You have no idea how much that means to me. How precious it is."

"I do know, Trevino, because it's how I feel when I'm with you. Even when you say I'll face 'consequences,' I'm not afraid. I know you'll take care of me, take care *with* me."

"I will, Eberly. I promise that I'll look out for you, keep you safe, and soothe you in the same way you do me. I'll protect and honor your body, your mind, and your emotions."

"I'll do the same for you."

"Now, we sleep."

She sighed. "If we must."

"Under the covers, little dove."

"Will you sleep next to me?" she asked.

"I will."

"Will you take off your clothes?"

Rather than answer with words, I pulled my shirt over my head with one hand while I unfastened my jeans with the other. After toeing off my boots and socks, I dropped my pants and shirt to the floor and crawled in beside her.

"I really want you to make love to me, Trevino."

"I want that too."

"But I understand why we're waiting."

"And then again, we're not. Feeling your skin next to mine is still making love, little dove. Every touch is that same expression of desire and caring. It's all love, Eberly."

When she didn't respond, I knew she'd fallen asleep. What I didn't know was whether she'd heard the most significant words I spoke tonight. Not only tonight, though, but the most important of my life.

15

Eberly

Yesterday, I'd fully expected that, when I woke up this morning, I'd no longer be a virgin. While I still was, the decision to put off intimacy felt like the right one.

How could I even think about it with my father missing? He'd been gone close to forty-eight hours, and I had no idea where to look for him. Given his best friend hadn't spoken to him in weeks and the last time his latest girlfriend saw him was the night of the ball, I was out of ideas. Adding in the argument I'd overheard him having on his cell phone, and his disappearance was distressing.

When I asked Trevino if I should contact Tiernan, he passed the question on to the sheriff, who said I should wait.

I was facing away from him, but since he was snoring, confirming he was still asleep, I wouldn't ask if that had changed yet.

It seemed logical that Tiernan showing up at the gate the same night my father disappeared was somehow related. That Trevino said his brother heard my ex-fiancé had played a role in my father selling Eberly Winery to the Wine Consortium made his relentless attempt to get me to open it suspicious.

Now, I regretted that whenever Tiernan and my dad discussed winery business, I'd tuned them out. I'd never had an interest in either making wine or growing grapes, which was surprising since I loved gardening so much.

When Trevino's hand moved from around my waist to my breast, I glanced over my shoulder at him.

"Good morning."

"That I woke up with you in my arms makes it better than Christmas." He nuzzled my neck. "How long have you been awake?"

"A few minutes." Desire pooled between my legs when his hardness pressed against my naked bottom. "Trevino?"

"Yes, my little dove?"

"Do you think maybe the first time…?" I wished I hadn't started the question, because once I said the words out loud, I realized what I was about to ask was the opposite of what Trevino had told me he needed as much as wanted. "Never mind."

"You'd rather it not be a scene."

"Sorry. I know—"

"I'd rather it not be too." He reached up and swirled my nipple with the tip of his finger, hardening it before switching to the other breast. "Roll to your opposite side so I can see you."

Our eyes met, and he cupped my cheek. "There's somewhere I want to take you today."

"Okay."

He rubbed my furrowed forehead. "Don't worry. I predict you're going to love it."

What I'd love would be for him to kiss me. Better yet. Put his hand between my legs—or his cock. I was in favor of being patient, but when a woman decides she's ready to lose her virginity, one would think a man interested in her would be as anxious to take it. Not that I'd say any of that since he made it clear we had to determine our *limits* first.

"Is there something you want to say to me?"

I shook my head.

"I sense you're frustrated."

There were at least five things on the tip of my tongue to say, but all were disrespectful. "Aren't you?"

He took my hand and wrapped it around his cock. "You can feel for yourself, little dove." He left his hand on mine and kept them both still. "Soon, I promise."

Unless it was in the next five minutes, whatever he was promising wouldn't be soon enough.

"Come. We can stop and pick up coffee and groceries on our way." He removed my hand from his penis and rolled away from me.

"Is whining permitted?"

He smiled. "Trust me. That's all I ask."

"Can I shower first?"

"Yes, but you can also wait to take one with me."

Now, I was intrigued. "Does it matter what I wear?" I didn't have much with me, so I hoped not.

"Wear something comfortable, but bring enough for a couple of days. Oh, and your work boots."

I kept a pair of Wellington rubber boots in the storeroom at the Stonehouse for the days when I worked in the garden.

We were on the road twenty minutes later, headed toward the ocean. I wanted to ask Trevino where we were going, but he'd requested I trust him, and honestly, I was enjoying the surprise.

When the main road that went from Los Caballeros to the beach ended, he pulled onto Cabrillo Highway and into the town of Cambria, where we stopped at the gourmet market on Main Street. I so rarely came down here anymore and hadn't realized how much I missed it.

"Hey, Trevino," said Louie, who owned the place, when we walked in. "Want me to have my son load your order?"

"Thanks," he said, stopping at the counter. "If it's boxed up, you can put it in the truck bed." He turned to me. "I stocked up, but if there's anything you're craving, let's get that too."

What I was craving had nothing to do with food. Although now that I thought about it, I was hungry. "Maybe some muffins?"

"You're in luck. The Olallieberry Diner dropped off our delivery a few minutes ago, and they're still warm," said Louie.

"Half dozen?" Trevino asked.

"Um, I'll eat one."

He smiled, then ordered three each of olallieberry and peach cream. "Coffee?" he asked.

"I can grab it," I offered. As I poured regular for me and decaf for him, I watched Trevino out of the corner of my eye. He'd lowered his voice and was saying something to Louie, who then smiled and nodded. "You got it," I heard the man say.

"Ready?" Trevino asked when I approached with our coffee.

"Whenever you are."

He leaned forward and kissed my cheek. "I can't wait to be alone with you, little dove," he whispered.

Sitting outside at a bistro table in front of the market, we finished our coffee. I ate one of the muffins while Trevino polished off two. As I was throwing our trash away, someone said my name. Spinning around, I came face to face with Tiernan.

"Hello," I said, thankful when Trevino stood beside me with his hand on the small of my back.

Tiernan glanced at him but didn't show any sign of recognition, nor did he speak to him. Instead, he stepped closer to me. "I've been trying to get in touch with you."

I raised my chin. "What about?"

He looked between Trevino and me a second time. "Could we speak privately?"

"Whatever you have to say—"

"I'm Trevino Avila. Who are you?"

I wanted to giggle at Tiernan's reaction. That was until his expression changed. "Is he the reason you called off the wedding?" he said rather than introduce himself.

My eyes scrunched. "What are you talking about?"

"It hasn't been that long, Eberly. Surely, you remember we were supposed to get married ten days ago."

"You were the one…My dad said…"

"Your father came to see me to tell me you'd had a change of heart and the wedding was off. I tried to call you, but apparently, you'd already blocked my number. I've also been by the house a number of times, but either you're ignoring me or are never there."

My mind reeled in confusion, but when Trevino moved his hand to my waist and held me tighter, I shook myself out of it. "We, uh, need to be going."

"That's it? You break off our engagement, and you have nothing to say to me?"

Trevino stepped between Tiernan and me. "Eberly owes you no explanation."

Tiernan sneered. "He speaks for you now?"

"Since I have nothing to say to you, no." I put my hand in Trevino's, stunned by the tension I felt seeping off him. "Let's go."

Since the truck was parked beside us on the street, we left Tiernan standing where he was, got in, and drove away.

"I'm—"

"Do not apologize."

"You seem angry."

We were a couple of blocks away from the market when Trevino turned on a side street, pulled over, and parked. "I am but not at you," he said, turning to face me.

"That conversation was so, err, bizarre."

"Do you think he's telling the truth?" he asked.

I didn't hesitate. "No."

Trevino put his hand on my leg. "Good."

"I realize now that there was a part of me that never trusted Tiernan. God, I can't believe I came that close to marrying him." I looked at Trevino. "I can't help but feel like there's something you're not saying."

"I don't have all the facts yet."

Chills spread through my body. "How worried should I be?"

His eyes bored into mine. "I promised you I'd keep you safe, and I will."

"Am I in danger?"

"I don't know for certain, but I'm not taking any chances."

I studied him, unsure what to think.

"I asked you before to trust me. Do you?"

Like I hadn't hesitated to respond when he asked if I thought Tiernan was telling the truth, I didn't now. "I do."

"Okay if we get on the road now? I'd rather have the rest of this conversation once we arrive."

"Of course."

He started the truck but kept his hand on my thigh. That alone brought me comfort.

Once on the road, Trevino went the way we'd come, but instead of turning east to return to Los Cab, he continued south for a few miles. Shortly after the highway veered inland, he turned right, in the direction of the ocean. The gravel drive curved in several places, eventually leading to a gate that looked more elaborate than the one we had.

Trevino slowed his truck, waited for it to open, then pulled through. The drive curved again, then wound its way up to a crest. Once there, he stopped and shut the engine off. In front of us was a sweeping view of the ocean.

"Where are we?" I asked.

"Technically, Harmony, but the unincorporated part," he said, looking out at the view like I was. "I've never brought anyone here, Eberly. In fact, no one knows about it."

"No one?"

He shook his head. "Not a soul." He looked over at me. "Whenever I imagined the two of us together, it was always here." He took my hand and brought it to his lips. "I hope you like it."

"I already do."

He started the truck, put it in gear, and as we made our way down the hillside, he told me about the place the former owners had named Poppy Hill Ranch.

"All together, around thirty-five acres." He motioned to the left. "Those are Valencia oranges, and beyond that grove, there are Star Ruby grapefruit." He turned his head to the right. "Those are avocado trees. All of it turns a decent profit."

He explained that the property was set up to be entirely self-sufficient with solar power, a deep well, and two ten-thousand-gallon storage tanks.

"In addition to the main house, there's a one-bedroom guesthouse that I haven't done much to yet."

"How long have you owned this?" I asked.

"Not quite a year." He shook his head and chuckled. "I guess if my family really wanted to find me, Ashford could've told them how to do it. Or maybe they decided not to bother looking."

"Were you hiding?"

His expression changed. "I guess you could say I was. More, I wanted to be left alone."

"Thank you for bringing me here, Trevino."

"I'd say it's my pleasure, but it will be yours too." He rested his hand on my thigh. "First, I want to show you around outside."

He parked near what he said was the main house. It sat at the highest point of the drive, so the views were breathtaking.

"By the way, it looks better on the inside than it does out."

"With the beauty surrounding it, one wouldn't even notice."

He smiled and held my hand as we walked down a stone pathway. "There's a greenhouse. That was the first thing I fixed up. Below that is the pond."

"Pond? It looks more like a lake."

"It's about three acres on the surface."

"Are there fish?" I asked.

"A few. I might stock it at some point." Once we got close to the water, he turned us so we were facing the house. "All this, I want to make into gardens like we did at the Stonehouse. Well, like you did."

I counted five separate areas that could be planted in addition to the raised beds that were in rows near the greenhouse.

"Seems like those would be perfect for a kitchen garden," he said, studying me as I took everything in.

"What's that?" I asked, pointing at another structure that looked like a garage but didn't have roll-up doors.

"I'll take you there later, but you won't believe it when you see it. It's a commercial kitchen, and it's huge."

I couldn't recall seeing Trevino as animated as he was while showing me around his property. "I like seeing you this happy," I commented while we walked up the path to the house.

"It's you."

I stopped and turned around to look at the views. "It's this."

He shook his head. "It's you being here with me."

Once inside the house, I saw how right he'd been about it looking much better than the outside. "Did you gut the place?" I asked.

"Basically."

The kitchen was state-of-the-art and very modern looking. The floors throughout were done in white oak, and the vaulted ceilings made the great room look massive. "I never would've guessed it was this big."

"We're talking about the room now or…?"

I rolled my eyes. "Yes, Trevino, the room."

"Too bad. Anyway, there are four bedrooms down this hallway," he said, pointing before leading me over to French doors. "This is one of the best parts." We walked out onto a deck that went the entire length of the house and looked out over the ocean.

"How do you ever leave?"

"It used to be harder." We walked to the opposite end of the deck, where there was a built-in hot tub.

Next to it were more French doors. "That's the largest of the four bedrooms."

"Will you show it to me?"

Trevino leaned up against the deck railing. "Last night, I told you that before we were intimate, I wanted to review our limits."

"Okay. We can do that."

"Actually, I'm going to propose something else."

I felt my cheeks flush but not in embarrassment. If he was about to tell me we still wouldn't be having sex, chances were good I'd push him over the deck railing.

He chuckled. "I'd love to know what you're thinking."

I folded my arms. "Actually, I don't think you would."

"Here's my proposal. The first time we're together, I want what happens between us to be natural. I don't want either of us to be thinking about control or limits or expectations."

"Are you sure?"

"Yes. I spent most of the night thinking about it." He stepped closer and pulled my arms apart. "I still want to introduce you to everything we talked about. But not today."

Today? I liked the sound of that.

He leaned forward and kissed me. "Now, I know what you're thinking."

"Yeah?"

He brushed my hardened nipple with his hand and stared into my eyes. "You are very transparent when you're aroused. I like that a lot, Eberly."

"I feel like I'm in a perpetual state of desire when I'm with you, Trevino."

He slowly closed his eyes, then reopened them. "If you'll let me, it's the way I want to keep you always. Ready for me, wanting me, open to me. When we're here, I'll want you naked all the time."

My breath caught. "Will you be naked too?"

"That's a conversation for tomorrow. In fact, the time for talking is over."

16
Bit

I opened the door, then led Eberly into the room and over to the bed. Like I had last night, I knelt between her legs. When I reached up to unfasten the flannel shirt she wore, she put her hand on mine.

"I can't believe I'm saying this, but is there food we need to put away?"

"Did you see any boxes in the rear of the truck?" I moved her hand and kept unfastening her buttons.

Her brow furrowed. "I wasn't paying attention."

"There weren't any. Sometime this afternoon, Benny, Louie's son, will deliver what I ordered and put it in the building where I told you there was a commercial kitchen." I leaned up and kissed her. "All I want you thinking about now is how you feel when I touch you."

Forcing myself to take my time, I removed her clothes until she was naked and sitting on the edge of the bed like she'd been last night. Then, I'd told her we'd hold each other but nothing else.

Today, my plan was to learn every inch of Eberly's body and how to wring pleasure from each place I touched. I'd use my fingers, hands, lips, tongue, and my cock, and then I'd start all over again.

"Where are we going?" she asked when I stood, took her hand, and led her toward a closed door.

"Remember what I said was one of the best parts of this place? It's got nothing on where I'm taking you next. Close your eyes."

I led her in so she was facing the most spectacular view in the entire house. Rather than the white oak I'd used in the other areas, the floors and two walls of this room were teak. The other two were glass. A circular tub, bigger than the one built into the deck, sat on a platform, and above it was a four-square-foot rain showerhead.

There were three doors built into the teak wall sections. Behind one were shelves with warm towels, another led to a dry sauna, and the other to the second area of the bathroom with two sinks, more teak shelves, and a water closet with a bidet.

Another door to the right of one glass wall opened to a separate deck with a daybed. There were heaters built in above and below it so the space could be used in both warm and cold weather.

The bed had other features Eberly wouldn't learn of today; however, my cock became hard as steel imagining her spread open and bound, powerless to do anything other than accept the pleasure I gave her.

"Eyes still closed?" I asked once I had her positioned for the optimum first impression.

"Yes."

I wrapped my arms around her waist and rested my chin on her shoulders. "Okay, open."

When she did, she gasped. "Oh, it's *gorgeous*."

While she looked out at the panoramic view of the Pacific Ocean, I moved one hand to her left breast and the other between her legs. "Open for me." When she did, I pressed between her folds and put pressure on her clit until she shuddered.

"Come," I said, leading her to the tub. When I pressed a button, water flowed from ports placed a few inches apart near the bottom around the inside of the bath. Each port had two openings. One button opened and closed the flow of water. The other emptied it. Because of the number of ports, it took under two minutes to fill.

Eberly turned in my arms. "It's spectacular, Trevino. I've never seen anything like it."

"Are we talking about the room again or…"

She put her hands on the waist of my jeans and pulled the five rivets loose, then pushed them down. "Not the room this time."

I shimmied, and they fell to the floor after I'd toed off my shoes and socks. I yanked my shirt over my head, and since I'd gone commando this morning, I was as naked as she was.

By then, the tub was filled almost to the top, but since there were overflow drains built into the floor, it didn't matter how much of a splash we created.

I lifted Eberly into my arms, lowered her into the warm water, then climbed in behind her. Once I was seated facing the ocean, she settled between my spread legs.

"You here with me is like a dream come true." I kissed down the side of her neck to her shoulder. "The things I want to do to you…"

"Like what?" Her voice was between a moan and a whisper.

She gasped when I reached between her legs and slid one finger into her wet heat. With my opposite hand, I pinched her nipple between my thumb and index finger and gently pulled. As I'd anticipated, her body arched, and I added a second finger, thrusting deeper.

"Can you come for me like this, little dove?" I curled the tips of my fingers inside her and rubbed her clit with the pad of my thumb. When she writhed, I held her steady with the weight of my arm. Her whimpers and cries of pleasure were nearly my undoing. While Eberly experienced orgasms by my hand, I'd held off, knowing nothing short of being inside her when I next came would truly satisfy me.

When the last threads of my restraint gave way, I removed my fingers, shifted her body away from mine, and got out of the water. I grabbed two towels from the warming closet and attempted wrapping one around my waist, but my painfully hard erection made it impossible. I quickly dried myself, offered my hand to help her out, then wrapped her in plush warmth before lifting her in my arms and carrying her into the bedroom.

I rested her on the bed, removed the towel from under her, then spread her legs. Her wide eyes met mine. "Tell me you want this," I groaned as much as said.

"I want everything with you, Trevino."

I leaned down and ran my tongue through her folds, making sure her body was soft and ready for me.

"I can't wait. I need you, little dove," I said, sucking her clit and easing my fingers inside her. As soon as her pussy clenched, I removed them, sheathed my cock in the condom I'd left on the bedside table, then positioned myself at her entrance.

"Eberly?" My eyes met hers, and I asked one more time if she was sure.

"Please, Trevino. Don't make me wait any longer."

I slowly pressed against her flesh, waiting until her body eased enough to allow me to go deeper. All the while, my gaze remained riveted to hers. Her quick intake of breath with my next thrust slowed me, but when she wrapped her legs around my waist, pressing me deeper, I thrust hard.

My cock pulsed as she clenched again, and I closed my eyes, willing myself back under control but knowing I wouldn't be able to if she made the slightest movement.

I reached between us, rubbing her clit with my thumb like I had a few minutes ago, slowly increasing the rhythm and depth of my thrusts.

When she cried out my name, I brought my mouth to hers, kissing her as the most powerful orgasm of my life left me shaking in her arms.

I held myself above her, not ready to withdraw from her body, and rolled us both to our sides.

"My precious little dove." I brushed her hair from her face. "I hope I didn't hurt you."

"If you did, the memory of it was obliterated by everything that came after." Her look of wide-eyed wonder made me smile. "Can we, um, do that some more?"

"That and so many other things." I eased my softening cock from inside her and rolled from the bed. "Do not move."

"Yes, sir."

"Keep that up, and we'll be doing more of it quicker."

I disposed of the condom, ran a washcloth under warm water, then returned to the bedroom. I spread her legs enough to gently clean her, then returned it to the bathroom. Before lying beside her, I took a second condom from the nightstand's drawer.

She glanced over at the foil packet, then at me.

"Do you have something you want to ask me?"

"You seem, err, prepared."

"Did you think I wouldn't be?" When her brow furrowed, I stroked her forehead with my fingers. "I told you earlier that I've never brought anyone else here. I did, however, dream of bringing you, and for that, I made sure I had everything we might need. Including sustenance," I added when her stomach rumbled. "Hungry?"

She laughed, and her cheeks turned red. "God, I'm so sexy, right?"

I cupped her face. "Everything about you is, Eberly." I leaned forward and kissed her temple. "Your eyes." Then the tip of her nose, then the corner of her mouth. I touched her bottom lip with my fingertip. "Your mouth, especially." I eased down her body and kissed across the soft flesh beneath her belly button, then rolled from the bed and pulled her up with me.

"Where are we going now?"

"I'm going to feed you so I can fuck you again."

"If you wanted to, ahem, *fuck* me first, I wouldn't mind."

I put my hand on her neck and kissed her hard. "Be careful, Eberly. I predict I will be insatiable when it comes to you."

She smiled enough that I could see a hint of her dimples. "Yes, please."

I'd brought the muffins inside earlier and had several other things in the refrigerator we could eat. "I'd offer to make you breakfast tacos, but they won't be anywhere near as good as yours were."

"I wouldn't mind making them."

My gaze traveled the length of her body, and my cock pulsed. Having her in my kitchen, naked, was almost enough to make me carry her caveman-style straight to bed.

"Is everything okay?" she asked.

"Maybe refraining from wearing clothes isn't the best idea when cooking," I said.

"You're probably right." She looked down at the floor rather than at me.

"Eberly?"

"I'll get dressed." She swept past me on the way to the bedroom, but I caught her around the waist.

"Is there something you want to say?" I asked.

"No."

"I've asked you to be honest with me."

She sighed. "I am being honest. You asked if there was something I *wanted* to say, and I said no."

I cocked my head. "You have me there."

"Look, I'm aware I don't know what I'm doing, and maybe I'm not as sophisticated as other women you've been with…"

"Do you think I'm passing some kind of judgment here?"

"Maybe."

"I'm not. I never would. Especially with you."

"But—"

We'd left our cell phones in the bedroom, and I could hear hers ringing. "This way," I said, leading her through the tub area. Once in the room, she raced over to answer it but was too late.

"It says the call was from an unknown number," she said, holding it out for me to see as her hand shook.

"Come here," I said, pulling her into my arms. "I'll contact Decker and see if he can figure out where the call originated from."

"He can do that?"

"Sometimes, from what I understand."

Rather than phone him, I sent a message with the time the call came in.

Roger that. I'll see what I can dig up, he responded.

"I feel like I should go home," Eberly muttered as she picked up the clothes that were lying on the floor.

"Of course," I said, doing the same and hoping she didn't suggest she stay there alone. If she didn't want me there, I'd call Michael Oliver.

Eberly put on her bra, shirt, and panties, then sat on the edge of the bed. "What if that was someone calling about my dad? Like a hospital?"

"If so, they would've left a message and would likely attempt to make contact again soon." The unknown number led me to believe it wasn't quite that innocuous.

"Let's get you home," I said once we were both fully dressed.

"I'm sorry. I know you wanted to stay longer. I feel so far away here."

"I get it, and I should've thought about that." The drive to her place from here would take close to an hour. I only hoped that whoever had called wouldn't try again in the next few minutes. It was another thing I should've considered. Cell coverage was spotty this far out and wouldn't get better until we reached the highway. "Your instincts are right in wanting to go home," I assured her.

"Trevino?" Eberly said when we were within a quarter mile of her house.

"Yeah?" I glanced over and saw she'd put her head in her hands. I pulled the truck over when I noticed her body shaking as if she was crying. "Talk to me, little dove."

"I'm scared," she whispered.

"Tell me what I can do to help."

"Can we go to the cottage instead?"

"Of course we can," I said, moving her hand from her face and cupping her cheek. "I'll take you wherever you want to go."

"I don't want to be alone."

I brushed her lips with mine, then smiled. "Did you think I planned to drop you off and leave?"

Eberly shrugged.

"Not a chance you'll get rid of me that easily."

"I don't want to get rid of you." Our eyes met. "Ever, Trevino."

I felt the same way. However, as recently as four days ago, we were nothing more than boss and employee. Once her father turned up and we were able to get her some answers, her dependence on me might come to an end. Allowing myself to think beyond that was too much of a risk. "Does knowing I intended to stay make you feel differently about going to the cottage?"

She shook her head. "Right now, I don't know if I can set foot in the house. Not even to get more clothes."

I'd tease her again about keeping her naked, but now wasn't the time, especially with the insecurity over it she'd expressed before we left my place. "I'll be with you, Eberly. Plus, my brothers have been overseeing upgrading the property's security system. If anyone comes or goes, we'll know. With the injunction and the winery being closed, there shouldn't be anyone here besides the vineyard manager and his staff."

"It isn't that. With everything my dad has done, I feel like I've been living with a stranger."

I took her hand in mind. "While I understand why you might feel that way, that house, even the winery, represents good memories too."

"You're right. It was a wonderful place to grow up. Like you said about Los Cab, I took it for granted."

"I won't pretend I know how you feel, Eberly. I cannot imagine how hard it is, believing your father has been dishonest with you. Worse, that it appears he committed fraud. What I do know is that holding on to good memories is what sometimes helps me get through the bad shit that's unavoidable in life." I wouldn't say it now, but there had been times when doing that kept me alive.

"So, house? Cottage? Clothes? No clothes?"

Eberly rested her head on my shoulder. "Thank you for being so sweet to me. Oh and, cottage, but I should pick up more clothes."

"You got it." I put the truck in gear and was about to pull out, but saw an SUV barreling in our direction. I turned the truck so it was farther off the shoulder.

"What is it?" She glanced behind us. "Oh my God." She grabbed my arm. "I think that was Tiernan," she said when the vehicle flew by us.

If Eberly wasn't with me, I'd follow, but there was no way I'd put her in danger. Instead, I sent a group text to the *caballeros*, then one to Vader. Both said the same thing.

Tiernan Burke spotted heading in the direction of Eberly Winery.

17

Eberly

Less than two weeks ago, I'd almost married a man who left me in a state of panic just by thinking I'd seen him in the SUV that passed us.

"Do you think he's stalking me?" I asked.

"I don't know, Eberly, but that we saw him earlier and again now is something the sheriff needs to know."

"Is that who you sent the message to?"

"Him and my brothers."

"Right. You said they were on the property."

Trevino didn't respond or even look at me, which wasn't like him.

"Is there something you're not telling me?" I asked.

"Not in the way you're thinking."

"In what way, then?" I pressed.

He put the truck in gear and pulled onto the road but turned around and went in the opposite direction of my house. "I'll try to explain once we're at Los Cab."

He'd *try* to explain? He wasn't making sense. I'd push harder, but since we were less than two miles from the entrance to the estate and winery, I'd wait. Once there, if he didn't explain sufficiently, I'd call my uncle and ask if I could stay with him and Aunt Evelyn. I'd had enough of people—my father in particular—keeping secrets from me. I couldn't accept it from Trevino too.

When he pulled in and parked, I was stunned to see my uncle, Michael, was already there, waiting. Zin was also with him.

"What's going on?" I asked.

"I'm not sure." Trevino got out of the truck, helped me down, then held my hand as we walked toward the cottage.

"Hi, Eberly. Uh, Bit, can we have a word?" Zin asked.

I tried to let go of his hand, but he held on tight. "Let's go inside," he said, motioning to them, then leaning closer to me as we walked up the porch steps. "I have to make one very quick call to my brother. It'll only take a minute."

He opened the door and led me over to the sofa. "Take a seat, guys," he said. "I'll be right back."

"How are you, Eberly?" Zin asked after Trevino left the room.

I folded my arms. "Tired of people not being straight with me." I looked between him and his father. Before either could respond, Trevino returned.

"I spoke with Brix. He's aware I intend to tell Eberly about the *caballeros*." Like I had, he looked between the two other men in the room.

"I think that's a good idea," said my uncle.

That seemed to surprise both Zin and Trevino.

"Earlier, I told you I sent a message to Vader and my brothers. Those words may have been misleading. What I am about to tell you, though, you cannot repeat to anyone else," said Trevino, sitting beside me.

"Okay."

"Do we have your word, Eberly?" Zin asked.

I could feel Trevino tense beside me.

"You do," I answered, squeezing his hand.

I listened as the three men told me about an organization they belonged to that had been in existence for hundreds of years. The way they explained it was that Los Caballeros, as it was called, was a secret society, a brotherhood of sorts, that came to the aid of those who needed help.

"I realize that explanation sounds vague," said Zin. "But it's accurate."

Trevino cleared his throat. "Last night, when your uncle stayed here with you, it was because I called an emergency meeting to discuss your father's actions and to see if anyone might know where he was. I shared the same things with them that I had with you about what Decker Ashford learned."

Like I had with him, he squeezed my hand.

"Go on," I said.

"Once Bit returned, that's where I went," my uncle added. "In conjunction with the sheriff, the *caballeros* are mounting an effort to locate your father. The other thing you should know, Eberly, is he's also a member. We consider him our brother, and we'll do everything we can to find him."

"Do you think something happened to him?" I asked.

"We don't know anything more than you do," said Zin. "However, we don't think he'd leave without telling you. Especially after the amount of time that's passed."

"The reason we asked for a word with Bit when you arrived is because another emergency meeting has been called." My uncle looked at his phone, then up at Trevino. "They're waiting for you now."

"I'll return as soon as I can," he said, squeezing my hand one more time before letting go and standing.

"Hold on," I said when he walked toward the front door. I rushed over and hugged him. "Thank you for telling me." I leaned up and kissed his cheek.

"You're welcome," he said, kissing my lips. "I'll try not to be long."

"Would you like a glass of wine?" I asked once my uncle and I were alone.

He stood. "I should probably stick with coffee if you've got it."

"I'll make a pot." I'd already had plenty, but something told me this would be a late night.

"With very few exceptions, only members are permitted to attend the Los Caballeros meetings. That's why Trevino didn't offer for you to go with him."

"It's okay. I get the impression that him even telling me about it was a big deal."

"It isn't allowed. I should rephrase that. Typically, once a *caballero* marries, there is an unwritten rule that their spouse be told about the organization. Not in every case, but most."

"Does Aunt Evelyn know?"

"Yes," he said, following me into the kitchen.

"I guess you all agreed to Trevino telling me since my dad was a member."

"I don't think that has anything to do with it. The way Trevino put it, I got the impression he told Brix he was making you aware of Los Caballeros with or without permission." He smiled. "I like the two of you together."

"I do too." How many times today alone had it dawned on me that marrying Tiernan would've been the biggest mistake of my life? "We ran into Tiernan today in Cambria."

My uncle didn't appear surprised.

"You already know?" I asked.

"An alert went out about both sightings."

"He said my dad told him I'd had a change of heart and called off the wedding. It was the same thing my dad told me, except in reverse."

"Do you know your mom and dad met through me?"

"I don't recall hearing that."

"Probably because he and I knew each other from Los Caballeros, and that means I've known your dad a really long time. While I have no explanation for his recent actions, I know in my heart that he wouldn't have done any of those things unless he felt he had no choice."

"Why didn't he talk to me about it? I could've helped. I still can."

"I can't speak for him, but my guess is he wanted to spare you."

When the electric kettle switched off, I poured the hot water over the ground coffee I'd put in the French press. "I'm not being spared now. It would've been so much better to hear from him."

"I agree, Eberly, but as your cousin said, we should give him the same benefit of the doubt the courts would."

"You're right. I'm just mad at him." I looked at the time. "How long do these meetings usually last?"

"It varies."

"Do you think someone has located him?"

Uncle Michael shook his head. "Trevino would've stopped the meeting to tell you."

I smiled. "You're right. He would have." I thought about him asking me to trust him. I did, and my quick response was evidence of it. I knew in my heart that if he had any news, he'd figure out a way to tell me as soon as he could.

"How did you meet Tiernan?" my uncle asked.

"At a wine industry event my dad asked me to attend with him."

"Did your father already know him?"

"If they'd met before, neither of them let on." I recalled how bored I'd been. When I agreed to go, I thought for sure Justine or Isabel would be there, but no one from our group of friends was. I'd gone to get a plate of hors d'oeuvres when Tiernan struck up a conversation with me. I remembered thinking he was handsome and a good conversationalist. He'd asked for my number, and while I doubted I'd hear from him, he'd called the next day and asked me on a date.

"I keep wondering if there were signs I should've picked up on."

"Do you mean with your dad or with Tiernan?"

I shrugged. "Both." I shook my head and smiled. "The other day, I remembered having a conversation with my mom about Trevino. At the time, she said he was her favorite of the Avila boys."

"She was a good judge of character."

I looked up at him. "Apparently not."

Uncle Michael shook his head. "What I'm saying, Eberly, is that she *was*, and we should keep that in mind in regard to your father."

"I wish I could. More, I wish he'd get in contact with me."

"Did you say anything about your dad when you ran into Tiernan?" he asked.

"No. I wasn't sure if I should."

"It was probably the right decision."

"Are you sure about that?"

His gaze hadn't appeared to be focused on anything in particular, but he abruptly looked at me. "At the time, yes. However, I'm wondering if you should arrange a meeting with him. One where we could listen in."

"You mean like wear a wire?"

"Something like that, except it isn't done that way any longer."

I almost asked how it was done, but decided I really didn't want to know.

18
Bit

"What have you been able to find on Tiernan Burke?" I asked as soon as Brix called the meeting to order.

"He doesn't exist," said Snapper.

"So who the hell is he?"

"Definitely someone associated with the Killeens," Snapper added. He pulled up footage from over a year ago, before the FBI raid. The surveillance video was grainy, like what Vader got from the gate at Eberly's place, but there was no question the man on the screen was the one we ran into in Cambria earlier today.

"Whoever he is, he's flown way under the radar," said Brix. "Have you read Decker's message yet?"

I hadn't, and I appreciated that, this time, he asked. I dug my phone out of my pocket and opened the app he used to send messages containing sensitive information.

While Ashford said he was still working on an ID, he found enough facial recognition hits to place him with known associates of the Killeens on more than one occasion.

"You don't think he's an informant, do you?" I asked.

"I'll run it by Ashford, but if he was, I would think he would've found him in the system."

I murmured my agreement.

"Let's say he is part of the organization," Snapper began. "How was he able to elude the feds, and what's his plan now? To put the Killeens back in business?"

"Everything they were involved in is still out there—drugs, weapons, extortion. It's a matter of time before either someone affiliated with the Killeens or a rival organization is able to get the cash flowing again," said Kick.

Brix looked over at Zin. "Do you still have a guy on the inside at the bureau?" he asked.

"Not a guy. My cousin."

"On Eberly's side of the family?" I asked.

"Yeah. He's my uncle's son. David is my dad's and Aunt Belinda's brother."

"Is this cousin clean?" Kick asked.

"Breck? Hell, yeah," said Zin.

"What are you getting at, Kick?" I asked.

He shrugged. "Maybe Eberly was targeted."

I glanced over at Zin, who appeared lost in thought.

"Why her, though? Because Malcolm was vulnerable? In Paso Robles alone there are plenty of wine heiresses with bank," Snapper added.

I kept my eye on Zin. There was something he wasn't saying.

"Not the kind of bank Eberly has," he finally looked up and said.

"How much are we talking?" Kick asked. "Ow! Fuck. Why'd you kick me?" he said to Snapper.

"Because you don't ask questions like that."

Zin's eyes met mine. Whatever the number was, it was significant.

"Could someone have gotten to Breck?" I asked.

He shook his head. "He wouldn't have willingly divulged anything about our family."

"Key word is willingly," said Snapper.

"Okay, let's say there's something to this theory," said Brix. "Burke's got a guy on the inside at the bureau—I'm not saying it's Zin's and Eberly's cousin—but he somehow got advance knowledge of the raid. Which explains how he avoided arrest. But how would he have found out Eberly's net worth?"

"Beginner hacker could get that info," Kick muttered.

I looked over at Brix.

"What are you thinking?" he asked.

"Everybody always says the Irish mob families don't lay claim to those in the US. But I doubt they'd leave money on the table if they saw a way to sweep in and take it for themselves."

"Are you thinking this Burke guy is a scout?"

"Possibly. Or he's an independent looking for investors."

"How many zeros are we talking she's worth, Zin?" Brix asked.

"High nines."

My brother looked at me. "How long were Eberly and Burke engaged?"

"How the fuck would I know?" I snapped.

"About a year," Zin answered.

"The FBI investigation took place over a period of five years," I said under my breath.

"So you're thinking Burke, or whoever the hell he is, knew about the investigation, knew there'd be a sweep of both the Killeens and FAIM, and was biding his time?" Snapper asked.

"And building his cash reserves," Brix added. "Takes drug money to make drug money."

"What better way to get your hands on an heiress' money than to sweep in and save the day after her father loses their business and home out from under her?" said Kick.

"He's got Malcolm."

Heads shot up around the table at my statement.

"Makes sense, Bit," said Brix.

I pushed my chair away from the table, rested my elbows on my knees, and lowered my head.

"Are you okay?" Snapper, who was sitting beside me, asked.

I shook my head and looked up at Zin. "Malcolm doesn't control her money."

"The question then is, does Burke still believe she does, or has he somehow found out it's my dad?"

"I'll send an update to Decker with our theory," Brix offered. "Is there anything else we need to address tonight?"

"There's got to be a connection between this guy and Grogan. As Ashford says, there are no coincidences. The similarity in their eye color is too significant to ignore," I said.

"Makes sense," Snapper commented. "If there is one, Burke would probably have insight into the Killeens income streams."

"And their street-level crews," Kick added.

I knew both my younger brothers had been doing contract work for people like Decker Ashford, but until now, I hadn't realized how immersed they'd gotten. For years, they'd been ranked team ropers on the rodeo circuit who were typically in the top five annual earners.

"You guys goin' to National Finals Rodeo this year?" I asked. The week-long event took place in Las Vegas in December, but in order to attend, individuals and teams had to qualify.

"Wouldn't miss it," Snapper muttered, studying something on his phone.

"What's up?" I asked.

"We've been monitoring various CCTV footage—"

"No one calls it that anymore," Kick interrupted.

Snapper glared at him. "Fuck off."

"Knock it off, boys…" Brix sounded so much like our father. It was eerie. "Snapper, go ahead with whatever you were about to say."

"Hughie Havers, Eberly Winery's vineyard manager, met up with Burke yesterday."

"Where?" I asked.

"The Grill." He handed his phone to me, and I replayed the video that showed the two walking into the local hangout. The next one showed them leaving within a couple minutes of each other about an hour later.

"Keep your eye on the motherfucker," I seethed, hating that someone who worked for her family was connected to a person we believed had ties to an organized crime syndicate. However, I also understood the importance of keeping him around for the time being.

"Anything else?" Brix repeated.

I understood his impatience. Addison, his wife, was pregnant and, from what he'd said, was expected to go into labor any minute.

When no one indicated there was more to discuss, he adjourned the meeting.

"I'll walk out with you," I said when I saw him heading toward the door. "Listen, I'll send the update to Decker."

"Sure. Of course. Sorry, Bit."

"For?"

"Turning into Dad."

I chuckled. "You channeled him pretty damn well when Snapper and Kick got into it."

He laughed too. "You're a good brother, Trevino, and a good man. I feel like I'm just now getting to know you, and I can't tell how bad that makes me feel."

"Don't waste your energy."

He glanced over at me.

"If you and Addy have a boy, name him Trevino." I winked and he laughed.

When I returned to the cottage, Michael was sitting in a chair, reading, and Eberly's eyes were closed. He stood silently and walked out when I sat beside her.

"Hey," she said, stretching her arms over her head. She looked around the room. "How long have you been back?"

I put my arm around her, and she snuggled into me. "A couple of minutes."

"I guess I dozed off."

"Let's go to bed."

"Okay, but…"

I raised a brow, and her eyes scrunched.

"What?"

"If you have something to say, say it."

Her cheeks flushed.

"Sorry, that came out harsher than I meant it to. I don't want you to feel afraid to say what's on your mind when you're with me."

Eberly put her arm around my waist. "It isn't you. Since my mom died…I don't know…I guess you could say I lost my security blanket. Her love for me was unconditional."

Between her dad and her ex, it was easy to see why she was feeling insecure. "I'll always want you to say what's on your mind."

"I was hoping we could talk."

"Always."

It took her a few seconds, but then she sat up. "What happened during the auction Saturday night? Why did you jump off the stage? Brix said you thought you saw someone."

"I didn't think it."

She put her hand on my arm. "I know. I saw him too. I mean, by the time I noticed, I saw a man leaving and you following, but I didn't see his face."

"It was Tiernan."

"I had a feeling you were going to say that." She sighed. "Not that it explains why you reacted the way you did."

"Tell me what you know about what happened in the wine caves a year ago."

"Not much. I mean, I'd heard you were hurt."

"At first, I thought he was one of the guys who ambushed me that night."

Eberly's eyes opened wide. "Oh my God. Was he?"

I shook my head. "He looked similar enough that I reacted."

Her eyes darted between mine. "Will you tell me what happened?"

As much as I never wanted to relive the events of that night, I knew what it had taken Eberly to ask.

"To be honest with you, there's not much I remember. It was my job to monitor the security feeds, and that night, there was a breach." I rubbed my left temple. "More than one, actually. I was near the caves at the time, which is where the alert pinged from." I had to take a couple of deep breaths.

"You don't have to go on, Trevino. I'm sorry. I shouldn't have asked." I looked into her tear-filled eyes.

"It isn't easy, but I want you to know, Eberly. What happened that night is part of who I am."

She took my hand in hers and stroked it with her thumb.

"I'd unlocked the main gate that led into the caves and stepped inside the entrance when two men jumped me. I didn't see either of their faces, but I'll never forget staring into the eyes of the guy in front of me."

It would be easy to say that was all I remembered until I woke up in the hospital after being in a medically induced coma for a few days. I couldn't stop, though. If Eberly was going to be a permanent part of my life, which I wanted more than anything, she had to know as much as I could tell her.

"Tiernan's eyes," she whispered.

"Amber irises. I'll never forget the color."

Eberly put one of her hands on her stomach. "I can't believe how close I came to marrying that man. I mean, I know you said he wasn't who attacked you, but the idea that he's related to whoever did makes me sick to my stomach."

"They hog-tied me, then beat the crap out of me. The last thing I remember is something hitting me in the head. That's when I lost consciousness. I'm sure they thought they'd killed me."

Eberly shifted forward and wrapped her arms around me. "Thank God they didn't, Trevino. I don't know…" I used the pad of my thumb to wipe away the tears that streamed down her cheeks.

"We have a code to send via the security system if I needed to take a break. An alert would go out, and someone else would know to monitor the feeds until I returned. If my cell went out of communication, that code went out automatically. That was how my brothers knew I was in trouble and where to find me."

"Thank God," she repeated, this time in a whisper.

"I was in the ICU for a few days, but according to the neurologist who took care of me, the hit to my head didn't cause permanent damage. He says the migraines will become more infrequent and eventually stop completely. I'll admit I'm not too sure I believe him."

"Do you have one now?" she asked.

I shook my head. "The last one was the night of the auction." I took another deep breath. "I wasn't the only person attacked that night. Two other men broke into my ma's house, tied her up, and pistol-whipped her. Addy's mother, Peg, was staying with her at the time, and when she came to, Peg was gone. She'd been kidnapped. As it turned out, that's who they were really after. Trying to kill me just made getting to her easier."

She gasped. "Were they ever caught?"

"Eventually. We were able to figure out it was one of the vineyard workers who sabotaged the system, allowing the four men to get on the property. Turns out the guy was a meth-head and his addiction was why he finally agreed to talk. Maybe he had a reason to believe someone would give him a fix."

"I had no idea. I mean, there were rumors, but no one knew anything for certain."

"What Los Caballeros learned was the four men were connected to organized crime. Not long after everything went down, the FBI staged a massive raid on two gangs operating out of Central California. Among the two hundred and fifty people arrested were the men who tried to kill me."

"Are they in jail?" she asked.

"Yeah, prison. Not eligible for parole for another ten years."

"How is Tiernan involved?"

"We have theories but nothing confirmed."

"While you were at the meeting, Uncle Michael asked how I met him."

"How did you?"

"As I told him, it was at a wine industry event my dad asked me to attend with him."

"Did your father introduce the two of you?"

Eberly shook her head. "Tiernan started a conversation with me, and since I was otherwise bored out of my mind, I kept talking to him. He asked me out, I said yes. It got intense fast." She shook her head. "I was such an idiot."

I raised a brow.

"*Was*. I'm not anymore," she quickly added.

"I'll let that one go."

"I'm sure you have other questions."

I cocked my head. "Like?"

"Why an engaged woman was still a virgin?"

"I never thought about why."

"I know you're telling me the truth, because I also know you wouldn't lie, but really?"

"My subconscious chose not to care why."

"You know what's crazy?"

I raised a brow a second time. "How much time have you got?"

She rolled her eyes, something else I chose to ignore for now.

"You and Tiernan are the same age. He looks so much older than you do."

"There's another thing you should know about him. The name he gave you is an alias."

"How sad is it that none of this surprises me? What is his name?"

"We haven't been able to positively ID him yet."

Her eyes opened wide. "So, you're like law enforcement?"

I smiled and shook my head. "Not even close. What I should've said is the people we work with—men like Decker Ashford—haven't been able to yet." I shut my eyes and resisted rubbing my temple. "Listen, if you see him again, I want you to be particularly diligent about avoiding him, not engaging in conversation, and definitely do not agree to meet with him on your own."

"Uncle Michael suggested I meet with him but have you or someone else listen in."

I shook my head. "Not a chance. I don't want you coming within a hundred feet of him."

"If your intention is to scare me, it's working."

"I'm sorry, but in this case, I want you to err on the side of extreme caution."

Eberly's phone rang, and she gasped. *"It's my father."*

19
Eberly

My hands shook as I hit the button to accept the call. "Dad?"

"Eberly, sweetheart. It's good to hear your voice."

"It's good to hear your voice too. I've been so worried."

"I know, and I'm so sorry, Eberly."

"Where are you? I've been trying to reach you."

"I'm sorry that I had to go away for a while, but I promise I'm trying to make things right. I need a little more time."

"Dad, the bank is trying to take the house." Something in my gut told me not to tell him about the injunction with it or the winery.

"I need more time, sweetheart."

"Dad? Did you hear me? What am I supposed to do about the house?"

"Goodbye, sweetheart. I'll try to call again soon."

I stared at my cell-phone screen in shock that the conversation was over so quickly. I looked up at Trevino. While I hadn't put the call on speaker, he was sitting close enough to me to have heard the entire, brief conversation.

"I don't know what to say. It's like I don't know my own father anymore. It was so…*bizarre*, right?" I looked down and saw he was typing something into his phone. "What are you doing?"

He raised his head. "Trying to remember everything he said."

"Oh. Good idea. Well, it shouldn't be that hard to do since he didn't say much."

He held his phone out so I could see the screen. "Did I miss anything?"

"I don't think so," I said after skimming it.

"What?" he asked when I shook my head.

To say something about the conversation was bothering me was an understatement. I was angry, hurt, worried, and confused, but along with all of that, something wasn't sitting right with me. "I can't explain it."

He set his phone on the table and leaned forward. "Let's break it down. Is there anything your father said that was out of character for him?"

"Hmm. Out of character? I guess most of it was. Except…"

"What?" Trevino pressed.

"He called me sweetheart three times."

"Was it the number or that he said it at all?"

I studied him. "At all. How did you know?"

"Your reaction. Anything else?"

"He didn't directly respond when I brought up the house. I don't know. Maybe that wasn't out of character. Remember, I feel like I hardly know the man anymore."

"Decker is monitoring your incoming calls. I should've told you that sooner."

"It makes sense that he would." My eyes scrunched. "But why didn't you tell me?"

I could tell he'd heard me, but it took him long enough to respond that I wondered if he would. Finally, he shook his head. "I don't know."

Part of me hoped he'd say nothing, but I knew better. Except, inside, I knew it wasn't because he was keeping secrets from me. He wouldn't hurt me. Just like my mom never would. Or Uncle Michael. There were certain people who I trusted that much. If I had the guts to take a good, long look at my relationship with my father, to the point where I allowed the hurt in, I already knew I couldn't say the same about him.

I shook my head. "There's more you aren't telling me, isn't there?"

By his reaction, I knew I was right. He practically flinched.

"Tell me now, Trevino. Either that or…"

His head shot up. "Or what?"

"I *trust* you. Don't do this to me."

His eyes scrunched but he gave in. "While I have no proof, my gut is telling me something is off with that phone call. Next, I have a strong suspicion that Tiernan Burke, or whatever his real name is, is involved in one or both of the gangs the FBI raided last year. In fact, I think he's trying to take over their former territories."

"Is there more?" I asked.

"I don't know what you're worth, Eberly, and I don't want to know. My theory, and I'm not alone in this, is Burke wanted to get his hands on your money in order to fund his criminal activities. That's why he proposed; that's why he wanted to marry you. Something happened. I'm not sure what, but it made him realize things weren't going to go the way he'd planned, and that's why he called it off. Or maybe your dad had something on him, and that's how he convinced him to walk away. Except now, I believe Burke has your dad. He didn't just disappear. He's being held against his will."

"What else, Trevino?"

He took a deep breath. "Next, he's gonna come after you and maybe even your uncle, if he's figured out he controls your trust fund."

I should be lying on the floor in the fetal position, except instead, I felt oddly empowered. As though every word he'd said made me see things clearly.

"I'm in danger."

"I'll die before I let him get to you."

I felt the air leave my lungs, and I clung to him, trying to catch my breath.

"Eberly? What's wrong?"

"My dad said almost the same thing. 'I'd sooner die than let you get your hands on it or her.'"

"And maybe that's what happened. Maybe your dad went after him."

"Do you think Tiernan will kill him?"

He opened his mouth to speak, then shut it.

"Say it!" I demanded.

Trevino's eyes bored into mine. "If he hasn't already."

"But I just talked to him."

"Did you? Are you certain?"

I let his words settle in. He was right. I wasn't certain.

"Ashford's calling," he said when his cell rang.

"Go ahead."

"Hey, Deck. Eberly and I are both here. You're on speaker. Were you able to analyze the call?"

He cleared his throat. "I'll hand it to you, young Avila; you're gettin' smarter and smarter the longer you work with me."

"Cut to the chase, Deck."

"You were right. No question it's a deepfake."

"What's that?" I asked.

"It's more commonly used to describe videos that have been digitally altered by using deep-learning artificial intelligence," Decker responded. "In essence, it's used to make it appear like a person said or did things they never did. It's imperceptible unless the video, or in this case audio, is closely analyzed. It was apparent almost immediately that your father's side of the conversation was fake."

"How?"

"You can duplicate a person's voice but not their style, if you will. His voice lacked the inflection that would be inherent to what he was saying. In other words, it was too flat. Taking it a step further, it was easy to confirm by the number of imperfections in the audio signal. It's a byproduct of the process."

A few minutes ago, I felt empowered. Now, I started to shake. With every passing second, it got worse.

"Decker, I need to cut this short." Trevino ended the call, gathered me in his arms, and carried me into the bedroom. "Fuck, I wish we were at the ranch," he muttered, lying beside me after resting me on the mattress.

"Take me there."

He angled his head so our eyes met. "I'm not sure that's a good idea right now."

I wriggled out of his arms and sat up. "I need to get out of here, Trevino. I feel like I'm going to come out of my skin."

"It'll take us an hour to get there. Are you sure you want to do this?"

"I *can't* stay here. It isn't that there's anything wrong with the cottage. I'm…I don't know how to explain it."

"Okay. We'll leave now." Before Trevino led me out to the truck, he grabbed a blanket, which he spread out on the bench seat. He helped me climb in and sit in the center like I had every other time I rode with him.

I shivered with desire when he said, "Listen carefully, little dove. This is how tonight's going to go."

20
Bit

I knew what Eberly needed. What I wasn't sure of was whether she was ready for it. The way our conversation went on the hour-long drive would determine how I'd proceed once we arrived at Poppy Hill Ranch.

Two things would happen regardless of what the rest of the night looked like. Eberly needed to eat, followed by a soak in the tub. That the cottage had a single shower was the reason I'd said I wished we were at the ranch.

Once we reached the highway we'd remain on for thirty miles, I was ready to begin.

"Upon our arrival at the house, you will go inside, remove your clothing, and kneel where I tell you to while I make us dinner. You won't leave that spot, and there will be no talking." I glanced over at her. "Did you hear me, little dove?"

"Yes, sir." Her voice was breathy, and her eyes drooped, confirming I was on the right track.

"After we finish eating, you'll go into the bedroom and wait while I prepare the bath."

"Um, yes, sir."

"Is there something you want to say?"

"Do I kneel again while I'm waiting?"

"Yes. In fact, if you're unsure during a scene, you will not be punished for kneeling unless I've given you specific instructions otherwise."

"Yes, sir," she repeated.

"Unfasten your jeans and remove them and your panties. Fold both and set them on the seat beside you." I waited a couple of seconds, then cleared my throat.

"Yes, sir."

"Good girl. Are you warm enough?"

"I'm fine, sir."

"Open your legs, little dove. Are you wet for me?"

"I think so, sir."

"Touch yourself, then show me."

From the corner of my eye, I could see her spread her folds and use two fingers to do as I asked. When she tentatively raised her hand, I grabbed her wrist and brought it to my mouth, licking her essence with my tongue. "Put two fingers inside your pussy, but do not move them until I tell you to."

"Y-y-e-s, sir."

While she still trembled, now it was with need, want, and desire, rather than overwhelming fear. For the next few hours, I'd keep her from diving too deep into her head by taking away her choices.

"Press the pad of your thumb on your clit."

Eberly whimpered.

"How do you feel, little dove?"

"I need more, sir." Her body writhed as she pushed her fingers deeper.

"Give me your hands. Both of them."

She removed them from between her legs more slowly than I would've liked, but that she followed my directions was what mattered for now.

"I told you not to move them until I said you could."

I could feel her body shudder.

"Tell me, little dove, should there be consequences for disobeying me?"

"Yes, sir," she whispered.

"What should they be?"

"You should punish me, sir."

"How, Eberly?" By using her name, I wanted to bring her out of her lustful haze enough that she could imagine what I might do.

"You could, um, spank me?"

I pressed her palms down on my thigh and reached between her legs. As I expected, she was drenched. "Is that what you want, little dove?" I glanced over, and her eyes met mine.

"Yes, sir."

"Say the words."

Her fingers pressed into my thigh where her hands still rested. "I…oh, God…I want you to spank me."

"What else? Should I lay you on our bed, spread your arms and legs, then bind your wrists and ankles so you can't hide yourself from me?" I reached up and pinched her nipple when she closed her eyes and writhed, grinding her wet heat on the blanket. "You haven't answered me, Eberly."

She whimpered. "I want that, sir."

I removed her hands from my leg. "I want to see two of your fingers disappear inside you. Thrust them in and out until I tell you to stop."

As on edge as she was, I didn't doubt that it would take much longer than seconds before she made herself come.

"Stop," I said when I saw her thumb brush her clit. "Eberly?"

"Y-y-e-s, sir?"

"Are you ready to come?"

"I think so."

I grabbed her wrists and brought her hands to rest on my leg.

"What? I mean, why did you do that?" Her voice shook.

"Who controls your pleasure, little dove?"

"You do, sir."

"Should you question me?"

Eberly shook her head. "No?"

"Should you obey me?"

"Yes, sir."

Her eyes widened when she realized I'd pulled up to the gates of the ranch. "Do you remember what I told you to do once we're inside?" I asked while we waited for them to open.

"Remove my clothes and kneel where you tell me to."

"That's correct. Have you heard me say you can put your pants on?" I asked when I saw her reaching for them.

"No, but…"

I didn't speak again until I pulled up to the house and parked. "Finish what you were going to say."

Her eyes scrunched.

"Tell me, little dove, before your punishment gets much worse."

"Do you want me to walk up the steps half naked?"

"If it's what I want, what should you do?"

"I should obey you, sir."

I opened the driver's door and got out. "Put the blanket around you and scoot toward me." When she did, I lifted her in my arms and carried her up the path and into the house. I set her on her feet, watching as she dropped the blanket and removed her shirt and bra. After lighting the fireplace. I grabbed a pillow from the sofa and tossed it on the floor. As she knelt, I put the blanket around her.

"I'm going to make something to eat. What should you be doing?"

"Um, nothing?"

I folded my arms and raised a brow.

"Waiting here for you, sir."

"Good girl."

After turning on the lights in the kitchen, I took several items from the refrigerator and quickly chopped a red pepper, green onions, and mushrooms, then tossed them into the pan I set on the cooktop. I checked every few seconds to see if Eberly was fidgeting, but each time I did, she remained perfectly still.

I cracked four eggs into a bowl, added a dash of sour cream, then poured the mixture into the pan of vegetables. Once it was scrambled together, I tossed a handful of shredded cheese on top, then spooned it onto a plate and grabbed a fork before walking over to where Eberly waited. I sat on the fireplace's raised hearth and faced her.

When I brought a forkful to her mouth, she opened. I continued feeding her until half of what I'd made was gone, then I finished the rest.

"What is the next thing I told you to do, little dove?"

"Wait in the bedroom, sir."

I held out my hand to help her stand. "Keep the blanket around you, then drop it on the floor near the end of the bed and wait for me on your knees."

Eberly went in the direction of the bedroom, and I took the plate to the kitchen, entered the bathroom from the hallway on the opposite side and, once in the outer part of the bathroom, pressed the button to fill the tub.

"You look so beautiful," I said, seeing her on her knees in the precise place where I'd told her to wait. "Spread your legs as far as is comfortable, then rest your hands on your thighs, palms up." I waited until she was in position. "Whenever I tell you to kneel and wait for me, this is the way I want you to hold your body."

"Yes, sir."

"Do you remember your safe words, little dove?"

"Green, yellow, and red, sir."

"Good girl. Unless you need to use yellow or red, I want you to remain silent unless I ask you a specific question."

I smiled when she nodded but didn't speak. After turning the water off in the tub, I checked the temperature, then returned to where Eberly waited.

"Come, little dove," I said, holding my hand out a second time to help her stand, then lifted her into my arms.

Like the last time we were here together, I lowered her body into the warm water, but instead of having her sit between my legs, I faced her. "Technically, we've been in a scene since we left the cottage. Now, though, things will get more intense. If anything I do or ask you to do makes you uncomfortable, use one of your safe words." I smiled again when she didn't speak. "You're making me very happy by following my instructions, little dove." I took her hands. "Stand for me, then straddle my lap."

My steel-hard cock rested between her legs, and as much as I wanted to bury myself deep inside her, first, we'd talk.

"Eberly, tell me about your sexual history."

Her eyes opened wide, and her brow furrowed.

"You may speak freely now."

"Apart from what I've experienced with you, I have none."

"No stolen kisses, no boyfriends feeling their way up your shirt, pressing their thigh between your legs, allowing you to take your pleasure?

"Kissing, but nothing else."

"What about when you're alone? How do you satisfy yourself?"

"What do you mean?"

"Do you use your fingers? Sex toys? Do you watch porn?"

Her cheeks were as flushed and her breathing as labored as if she'd run a mile.

"Answer me, little dove."

Her eyes were downcast, but I sensed it was due to her embarrassment, not submission. "I've used my fingers."

"Nothing else?"

"I've, um, read books, sir."

"Thank you for your honesty. Have any of these books contained elements of BDSM?" I'd know immediately based on her reaction to the acronym alone.

"Yes, sir."

"And have you brought yourself to an orgasm when reading about it?"

Eberly shook her head.

"Why not?" I asked, assessing her physical responses to our conversation as much as the verbal ones.

"Because you told me that you are responsible for my orgasms. Only you."

My heart rate increased, and my already stiff penis throbbed. My control was held by the barest of metaphorical threads. I inhaled deeply, reminding myself that it was essential I take command of my body as much as hers. What we did in the next few hours would be about teaching Eberly about my needs, but more, to satisfy her cravings, give her pleasure otherwise unimaginable to her, and take away the hurt and fear learning about her father's and ex-fiancé's betrayal had brought—even if it was for a brief amount of time. It was up to me to take the utmost care of her emotionally, physically, and mentally, which meant my focus had to be entirely on the woman whose hardened nipples were almost close enough to taste.

"So prior to our time together, you didn't read books of that nature. Is that correct?"

"Yes, sir."

I smiled. "When have you had time to read, little dove?"

Her cheeks flushed. "I sneaked it in here and there. Mostly on my phone."

"In these books, were the women restrained? Punished? Were they spanked?" Her gaze remained downcast. "Look at me, little dove. Did it excite you?"

"One book and, yes," she whispered.

"Which is how you knew you might like to experience those things yourself when I asked."

"Yes, sir."

"What are some things you read that you didn't think you'd like?"

"Something harsher, like being whipped or caned." She shuddered. "Or being shared."

"I would never do any of those things with you. I'm not a sadist; I'm merely a dominant. As far as sharing you, if it was something you decided you wanted, it would have to be a hard limit for me. Meaning, I couldn't do it. What else?"

"There were things mentioned but not done that sounded horrifying."

"Blood play?"

"That was one. Also, fire play."

Rather than continue discussing things that would turn both of us off, I rested my hands on her hips and brought my lips to hers, gently caressing her mouth until she opened to me.

As I circled her tongue with mine and her thighs tightened, I nipped her bottom lip before leaning away. "Is there anything else you want to talk to me about or tell me now?"

"I don't think so, sir."

"I'm going to remove you from my lap, then you are going to sit with your hands at your sides while I take care of you. If there is anything else you need to say, do it now, little dove. Otherwise, only speak your safe words."

"Yes, sir," she whispered, easing her body from mine. I turned her in my arms and pulled her between my legs before grabbing body wash from a shelf built in near the edge of the bathtub. I ran my soapy hands over every part of her before turning on the rain shower above us. Its flow was slow and gentle but enough for me to wash her hair.

When finished, I shut off the rain shower, took her hand in mine, and poured body wash into her palm. After putting it away, I leaned against the porcelain and spread my arms and legs. Eberly smiled, then washed me in the same way I had her.

My desire for her had reached the point of being painful, so in an effort to move things along more quickly, I dunked my head under the water, drizzled shampoo into my hair, and washed it myself.

I stood, grabbed two towels from the warmer, opened the ports to drain the water, then held my hand out for Eberly to stand too. When her gaze landed on my erection and she didn't look away, I couldn't help but imagine her kneeling before me as I thrust into her warm and eager mouth.

"Dry yourself, then I will help you get out. Then go into the bedroom and lie face up. Spread your arms and legs for me, like you imagined when you read the stories. There is one more thing we haven't talked about that I'd like you to consider doing for me."

Her eyes met mine.

"I would like to blindfold you, little dove."

She nodded once, wrapped the towel around her, then waited for me to help her out. I gave her time to get herself in position and settled on the mattress before joining her. I stood at the end of the bed and spread her legs farther apart. Her eyes opened wide when I reached down and pulled a cuff attached to the footboard from where it was previously hidden by the bedclothes. I fastened it around her left ankle and moved up her body, trailing my fingers as I went, then cuffing both wrists and her other ankle. Next, I covered her eyes with a black silk scarf, tying it behind her head.

Kneeling between her legs, I ran my hands up the inside of her thighs, then leaned down and captured a hard pink nipple between my lips. I kneaded the opposite breast, then caught the nub between my fingers and tugged gently, before letting go and trailing my mouth and tongue down her center. She squirmed and writhed but was unable to move much beyond that, given her restraints. Alternating between her saturated entrance and her swollen clit, I licked and sucked, then added two fingers. Her pussy softened, growing wetter each time I thrust. When I curled my fingers and attached my mouth to her clit, Eberly screamed my name as she shook with the first of what would be many powerful orgasms I planned to give her.

When her pussy clenched my fingers, I couldn't wait any longer. I withdrew them from inside her, sheathed my cock, and positioned myself at her entrance, then buried myself as deep as I could with one thrust. Eberly cried out, and she tightened around me as if to hold me still. I couldn't. I'd been on the same edge she'd been far too long. Now was not the time for gentle lovemaking, I pounded into her, adjusting the angle, then rotating my hips before slamming in again as deep as her body would allow me.

"Come with me," I practically pleaded, knowing I couldn't hold on more than a few more seconds. Eberly cried out again as she convulsed in pleasure.

As soon as I felt her heart rate return to normal, I pulled out and caught the release on the wrist cuffs, one with each hand. "Keep them there until I tell you to move." I rolled from the bed, released the ankle cuffs, then put my arm around her waist and lifted her in my arms.

I sat on the edge of the bed, then shifted to put her across my lap. "Hold onto my legs and spread yours so I can see how wet you are," I demanded.

My cock pressed against her abdomen, and it was all I could do not to have her straddle me again, but this time, ease herself down and take her turn fucking me. First, though, her punishment.

Eberly whimpered as I kneaded and stroked the flesh of her ass.

"I am going to spank you now, little dove. Each time my hand connects with your bottom, I want you to count, thank me for it, then ask for another. You will take twenty from me."

"Oh, God," I heard her whisper. There'd come a time when her doing so would earn her an extra ten, but not tonight. Not her first time.

I flexed my fingers, raised my hand, and brought it down hard. She cried out in shock, her muscles tightened, but within seconds, she softened across my thighs.

"Eberly?"

"Um, one. Thank you, sir, and may I please have another?"

"That was beautiful, little dove."

One after the other, she followed my instructions. Some spanks were gentler, some more intense than the first I gave her. Her body shook as tears ran down her cheeks, but it didn't stop her from responding perfectly each time.

"We're halfway. What color are you, little dove?"

She took a deep breath and let it out slowly. "Green, sir."

She'd brought her legs together, but I spread them and thrust two fingers into her pussy. She was so wet that I wondered if she'd come while I spanked her. If not, she was about to.

"Trevino, please," she moaned.

"Tell me what you need, little dove."

"Please, sir, I need to come."

I switched fingers so I could reach her clit and curled those inside her while I squeezed her bottom, warm and a beautiful shade of red, with my other hand. I knew the combination of pain and pleasure would send her soaring, and I wasn't wrong.

"We are not finished, little dove. Are you ready to continue, or do you need to use your safe word?" I asked when her body went limp.

"Please continue."

"That will earn you one more."

Again, she whimpered. *"Please, sir."*

"Good girl." I brought my hand down again, increasing the pace to the point where it was difficult for her to count, thank me, or ask me for another before the next landed. The last three were harder than any that came before them, and by the time I stopped, Eberly was sobbing.

I helped her stand, turned down the sheet and blanket, then placed her under them. I crawled in beside her and held her in my arms as she cried.

"Let it out, Eberly," I soothed. "I want to hear you."

She breathed in, and when she released the air she held in her lungs, I held her close to me, stroking her hair, her cheek, her soft skin. It took several minutes, but eventually, her sobs subsided and she opened her eyes.

"Did you do all that just to make me cry?" she asked.

"No, little dove. It was to get you to release everything you held inside. To allow the pent-up pain to escape, to cleanse yourself from the hurt."

"I feel…different. Lighter."

"As do I. Punishing you, little dove, isn't easy on me. It hurts my heart as much as my hand connecting with your bottom hurts you."

"But you knew I needed it," she whispered. "Thank you, Trevino."

"Thank you, my love."

Neither of us spoke for several minutes, and by then, Eberly was sound asleep. I pulled the blankets over us, and slept too.

21

Eberly

At some point in the night, Trevino woke me, put me on my hands and knees, and took me from behind. After giving me two more mind-blowing orgasms, he gently rubbed cream on my bottom, then told me to go back to sleep.

When I woke and saw the sun was up, I felt like I'd gotten my first good night's rest since before my wedding to Tiernan was called off. Actually, longer than that.

I stretched my arms above my head and smiled, knowing my entire body would be sore today, but it was worth it.

"She's awake," Trevino said, coming and sitting beside me on the bed. "And she's smiling." He leaned down and kissed my forehead. "How do you feel?"

"My answer now would be amazing. When I try to get up and walk around, I might change my mind."

"A warm bath will help. Followed by a good rubdown."

"Both sound like heaven."

Trevino moved the sheet that covered my breasts down to my waist, and the only ache I could feel was between my legs, and that was one of desire.

"Let me look at you. Hands at your sides, and do not move or speak." He focused his attention on my chest, using his hands, fingers, lips, and tongue to bring me to the point where I wanted to scream at him to give me what I so desperately needed.

"Come, time for breakfast," he said, pulling the sheet so it no longer covered me.

Something told me not to spread my legs the way I wanted to or grab his hand and bring it to my pussy. No doubt, it would bring me another spanking, and while that sounded good, I doubted it would feel that way.

When he stood and held out his hand, I took it, thrilled when he pulled me into his arms, caressed my cheek with his fingers, and kissed me.

I'd never dreamed the way he made me feel was possible. It was as though he knew me so well he could give me what I needed long before I realized it myself.

"Thank you," I said when he rested his forehead against mine.

"You're welcome. Let's eat."

While he wore no shirt, socks, or shoes, he did have on a pair of well-worn jeans that were sexy as fuck.

"Should I, um…" I motioned to my nakedness with my hand.

"Use your words, Eberly." His expression was hard to read.

"Should I get dressed?"

"Are you cold?"

I thought about it for a couple of seconds. "No, not really." He raised a brow but didn't speak. "So I guess I shouldn't."

"I've said more than once that you're welcome to tell me if something you're doing or I've asked you to do makes you uncomfortable. Unless you use the word red, it may or may not stop whatever is happening. However, I will listen to both your words and your body's responses."

"Are we in a scene now?"

"We are not. However, I want you to be naked and available for me to look at and touch whenever I want to, little dove. Tell me, is your pussy wet?"

I didn't need to check. I knew it was. "Yes."

"Perhaps what you really desire is for me to tell you to remain naked."

"I do," I confessed.

"What else do you want, Eberly?"

"I want you to touch me."

His eyes blazed. "Where?"

I reached out and put my hand in his. When he didn't pull away, I brought it between my legs.

With his free arm, he unfastened his jeans and let them drop to the floor. He turned us around so he lay on the bed. "Get on top of me and put my cock in your pussy."

I had to grip the mattress when I was certain those words alone would be my unraveling. I took a couple of deep breaths, climbed up on the bed, then straddled him.

"Now, little dove." He sounded as on edge as I felt, easing myself down on his hardness.

"Oh, God," I moaned when it felt deeper than it had been before.

"Fuck me the way you like me to fuck you."

He kept his hand on my waist to steady me as I increased my pace, eased off him, then thrust down. I *loved* it when he did that to me.

I was close to having another orgasm when Trevino flipped us both over. He pulled out of me, grabbed a condom from the bedside table, and in what seemed like mere seconds, he'd put it on and was inside me again.

I wrapped my legs around his waist and put my hands on his shoulders, digging into his flesh with my fingernails when I felt like I was ready to burst. He stilled when I squeezed him with my pussy, pulsing inside me. "God, Eberly," he groaned as much as said. "It's never been this good."

Warmth spread through me. "Really?"

Trevino kissed me. It was long, hard, and deep, answering my question far better than words ever could.

"There are many things we need to discuss today," Trevino said when we sat on the deck, eating breakfast after he gave in and allowed me to get dressed.

"My father," I said, taking a spoonful of yogurt, granola, and fruit. "Tiernan. My house. The winery. Does that about cover it?"

"Close. There is also the matter of your protection. I would like to ask Los Caballeros to set up a schedule so there are at least two people with us at all times."

I choked on my coffee. "With us?"

"I meant on the property when we're here or anywhere, really."

"Do you really believe I'm in danger?"

He sighed and rested against the chair. "I'm confident that today will bring at least some answers. Our priorities are to find your father and learn the real identity of Tiernan Burke."

"Do you believe my dad's alive?"

Trevino reached across the table and took my hand. "I do, and there are several reasons why. Something more is at play here, and while we don't know for certain, the most obvious would be that Burke pursued a relationship with you due to your family's wealth. At the same time, your father was facing financial difficulties that began with your mother's illness and the medical expenses he incurred."

"Compounding it was the pandemic, followed by a drop in wine sales further exacerbated by overproduction," I added.

"What else?" he asked.

"I can't explain it, but I don't believe my father willingly mortgaged the house or sold the winery. Even if he felt up against a wall, he would've asked for help. I can't believe he'd destroy everything our family built over decades in five years."

Trevino squeezed my fingers. "I think you're right, and it makes me happy to hear you're giving Malcolm the benefit of the doubt."

"It's amazing how great sex followed by the best sleep I've had in weeks has given me the clarity I didn't possess twenty-four hours ago."

He smiled and brought my hand to his lips. The love I saw in his eyes warmed me all over. It was love, wasn't it? As crazy as it sounded, it had to be.

"Trevino, I…"

"We are going to work on your inability to finish your sentences." He sighed, but winked. "Let me think. What would be a good consequence to help break you of the habit?"

My mouth gaped. "Are you serious?"

"Half." He took a bite of the muffin he'd warmed for himself.

"Half what? Serious?"

"Tell me what you stopped yourself from saying."

"It was—actually, I stopped myself on purpose that time."

"Tell me," he repeated.

I counted to seven while taking in a deep breath. "I like you. A lot."

"Come over here." He tugged me to his lap. "You like me *a lot*?"

"Yes."

He chuckled. "I, on the other hand, remember the exact moment I fell in love with you."

"You love me?" I gasped.

"Eberly, please. There are many things in your life you can't be sure of. Me? How I feel about you? My *love* for you. It's an absolute."

"I, um, don't know what to say."

He leaned forward, and I could feel his warm breath on my ear. "Be honest with me about your feelings," he whispered.

"I remember the exact moment I fell in love with you." I rolled my eyes. "Of course, you don't even remember meeting me that day."

"Tell me about it."

"Will you tell me when you fell in love with me?" I asked.

"Of course. But you first."

"It was right after crush. I think I was maybe seventeen. Los Caballeros was hosting the harvest party that year, and—"

"You were sitting on the ground under the big white oak tree. Your legs were crossed, and you were running your hand over the grass."

My eyes opened wide. "I was so bored."

Trevino shook his head. "You were feeling left out of the festivities."

"I was. Everyone was dancing, even Isabel, who at the time was the epitome of an ugly duckling. Sorry, I know that isn't nice."

He winked. "Isabel isn't nice."

"I saw you walking in my direction and was sure you'd go right on by. I even looked over my shoulder to see whoever it was you were on your way to talk to."

"I took your hand and pulled you to your feet—"

I smiled, but my eyes also filled with tears at the memory. "And we danced under the twinkling lights."

"For the first time."

"I thought you didn't remember."

He put his arms around me. "And now I do. Is that why you insisted we string them in the old winery?"

My cheeks flushed. "I've dreamed of dancing with you again ever since that first night, and it's always under those same lights."

"All it took for you to fall in love with me was dancing?" He grinned.

"You know it was so much more than that." I brushed away the tear that slid down my cheek. "That night, I told my mom I'd marry you someday. She put her arm around me and told me you were always her favorite Avila boy."

Trevino frowned. "The timing wasn't right for us then."

"I was a *kid*."

He chuckled. "And I was a man." He cupped my cheek and turned my head so we faced each other. "Say it, Eberly. Let me hear the words."

"I love you, Trevino, and I'm sorry—"

He cut me off with a passionate kiss. "I love you, Eberly, and I'll never be sorry for it."

"I almost married another man."

He shook his head. "You never would've gone through with it."

"No?"

"Even if you made it to the church, before you put your arm in your father's and walked down the aisle, you would've thought about the day we danced in the old winery, and you would've known you couldn't possibly feel that way dancing with anyone but me."

I giggled. "You're right. I would've hitched up my wedding dress, dashed out of the church, and begged someone to bring me to Los Caballeros."

"We were meant to be, little dove."

I rested my head on his shoulder, closed my eyes, and prayed he was right, prayed this would never end and Trevino and I would spend our whole lives together. It seemed too good to be true.

22
Bit

Even as I said the words—that while many things in her life were uncertain, my love for her was absolute—I knew it could never be that simple. I did love her, and I always would, but could that be enough for her and for me?

The darkness I'd felt for as long as I could remember too often overshadowed everything else in my life. I'd never been a rainbow-and-sunshine kind of guy, and regardless of how much light Eberly filled my life with, my depression would eventually eclipse it. It was as inevitable as the tide turning.

Last night, while she'd slept soundly, I was plagued by overwhelming anxiety. The feeling that something horrible was about to happen spread throughout my body. Taut muscles, heaviness on my chest, and dread in my stomach made sleep impossible.

In moments like these, when it was so easy for me to share my feelings honestly, I lamented that it wasn't always possible, let alone simple. If Eberly woke in the middle of the night to find my eyes wide open and she asked what was wrong, I knew without any doubt I would've lied and said it was nothing.

I was ashamed that I'd tried to assuage my pain through sex when I woke Eberly and took her from behind. I was proud of her when I'd gotten rougher than I was and she'd said, "Yellow." When I confirmed she only wanted to slow down, she assured me she knew when to use the word red.

"Are you okay?" she asked, raising her head from my shoulder.

"Don't ever forget I love you."

"I won't. Don't you forget, either."

The natural supposition was she meant not to forget she loved me. Except my first thought was about my feelings for her.

As I'd told Eberly a few minutes ago, my plan was to set up round-the-clock security for her today. I'd learned a lesson a year ago, and that was, regardless of how tight I believed security was at Los Cab, here, or anywhere, there would be holes that those with evil in their blood could find.

Part of me wanted to take her to Tryst's ranch. While it wasn't any more secure than this one, it was hours away, in Mexico.

"I feel like you're having a conversation with yourself."

I chuckled at the accuracy of her statement. "Sorry, little dove. Your safety is at the forefront of my mind this morning."

"Do you think we could go to my house today? I'd like to pick up some more clothes and maybe a few other things."

"Of course." I tried not to let her see the trepidation I felt over leaving this ranch. Eberly wasn't a prisoner here, and I certainly didn't want her to feel as though she was. "I'll call Snapper and let him know we're on our way."

I could feel Eberly's tension increase when we were within a mile of her house. "There was a time I wasn't sure I could return to the wine caves."

"How long did it take you to get over it?"

"I still hate walking past the room where the attack happened, but it gets easier each time I do."

"You were attacked and left for dead. My phone rang a bunch of times at midnight. Vast difference in experiences." Eberly was facing the window, so I couldn't see her expression.

"Who did you learn that from?" I asked.

"What do you mean?" she asked, turning toward me.

"Which of your parents discounted their feelings?"

She shrugged. "My dad, I guess. From him, I learned to be a realist and to believe in magic from my mom."

I pulled up to the newly installed gate, entered the code Snapper sent me, then drove through.

"That closes fast," Eberly commented, looking behind us.

"Its sensors are set to once a vehicle has safely crossed," I muttered, noticing Snapper walking in our direction. The look on his face was one I was familiar with; I'd seen it in the mirror often enough. He was frustrated enough about something that, with every step he took in our direction, his expression darkened.

"Give me a minute before we go inside," I said to Eberly after walking to open her door.

"What's up?" I asked when my brother got closer.

"Nothin'," he muttered, looking off in the distance.

My mouth gaped. "If whatever you're pissed off about will affect Eberly in any way—"

"It won't. It's some ropin' shit with Kick."

My two youngest siblings had been joined at the hip from the time they were kids. In fact, they looked and acted so much alike that most people thought they were twins. They weren't. Two years separated them in the same way it did Snapper and me.

"Is he here?" I asked since I had expected he would be.

"Yeah, he's here." He sneered.

"We'll talk later," I said, motioning to where Eberly sat, waiting for me—to go into her own house. How fucked up was that?

I knew something serious was up when, rather than protest, Snapper thanked me.

"Hey. Sorry," I said. "Ready to go in?"

"No problem, and I guess so." Eberly took a deep breath, put her hands on her hips, but didn't take a step forward.

"We don't have to do this now."

"It isn't that I'm afraid or anything. It's more that wherever I look, something will remind me of what my dad did."

I took her hand and led her over to a bench that sat in the middle of the garden that was planted in the middle of the circular driveway. "Tell me about this," I said, motioning to the flowers and other plants.

She surveyed the space, and gradually, her expression turned from a frown to a smile. "My mom and I started this butterfly garden when I was a young girl. I might've been ten. I can't remember exactly. We worked on it all the time, until she got sick. Then she'd come out with me and sit where we are while I weeded and deadheaded." She chuckled.

"What?" I asked.

"She took great pleasure in ordering me around while I did."

"Are there other gardens the two of you planted?"

"Many, actually."

"Will you show them to me?"

Her eyes lit up. "Of course."

"I see where you got the idea for the kitchen garden," I said when we walked to the side yard that was off that part of the house.

"She and I used to make dinner together, and we'd come out here and get fresh vegetables and herbs to use. Sometimes, we'd base the whole meal around whatever was ripe." Eberly smiled again. "It drove my dad crazy when he'd return to the house after spending the day in the winery to find what he called 'rabbit food' instead of a real dinner."

We continued around to the opposite side of the house, where a rock garden bordered one side of the patio with flagstone steps leading up to a seating area.

"We could go in this way, unless there's more you want to show me," I suggested.

"Most of the rest were around the tasting room and winery." Her eyes scrunched. "I don't have a key."

"Right. Hang on." I sent a text to Snapper, who came around the corner of the house a few seconds later. Like earlier, his expression troubled me. There had to be something else going on besides a disagreement between Kick and him.

"I need to give you an overview of the new security stuff that's been added, but you won't need keys any longer. Everyone with access to the house will have a unique code, which you'll determine now. It needs to be three letters and three numbers, none consecutive, and nothing too obvious."

"Like my birthday?" Eberly said, rolling her eyes. "I swear that's the only code we've ever used for anything."

She wasn't watching Snapper, but I was. Something about what she'd said made him flinch.

"Once everyone's set up, I'll get rid of my code. I have it now so I can do the programming and testing," my brother explained. He looked between Eberly and me. "Let me know if you, uh, want anyone else to have access."

She looked confused for a minute, but then it dawned on her what he was asking. "I definitely want Trevino to have access."

"Are you sure?" I asked.

Her eyes widened but not in surprise. She blinked several times and looked away. "If you don't think it's appropriate, then…"

"I mean, I'm happy to, err, honored, really."

Snapper nudged me. "Give me your code."

"Hang on," I said when Eberly punched hers in and was about to go inside. Something felt off to me. "Let me go ahead of you."

She stepped aside, and I walked in.

"Someone's been in here," she said once we were a few feet beyond the door. She looked at Snapper. "Was it you?"

"I haven't been in this part of the house."

"Tell me what makes you think someone was," I said.

She grabbed my arm. "It was Tiernan."

I put my arm around her waist. "Why, Eberly?"

"His cologne. Green Irish Tweed, it's called." She shivered. "I've always hated it."

"Do you want to return outside?" I asked.

"Let's go into the other room instead," Snapper suggested.

Once in the living room, he asked us to take a seat. "We did see someone on the surveillance footage entering the house through a walled-off area on the east side."

"The secret garden," said Eberly.

"While most of the property was wired, there were areas that hadn't been completed yet. By the time we got over here, whoever it was, was gone."

I was seething. "When was this?"

"Zero four hundred, err, four this morning."

I let go of Eberly's hand, stood, and walked to the other side of the room. I got why he wasn't elaborating. He didn't want her to freak out. My problem was that that I hadn't been informed of it until now.

"We've had a crew here since then," he said when my eyes bored into his. "The first thing that was secured was the house."

"By whom?"

"Ashford."

"He's here?" My fists clenched. It was another thing I hadn't been informed of, and why the fuck not?

"Some was done remotely, but, yeah, he's here."

Snapper had more to say, but wouldn't now because of Eberly; that much was clear. Except this was her house and her life.

"Start at the beginning. A person, whose identity you haven't yet determined, gained access to the house at approximately four this morning. Is that correct?" I asked.

"Yes."

"Was there footage of him leaving the house?"

"Yes. About ten minutes later."

"Who responded to the breach?"

"A couple of Vader's guys and Kick."

I leveled my gaze at him. Did this have something to do with why he and Snapper were at odds?

"What did they discover?" I asked.

"He left through the vineyards. Bit, it wasn't possible for us to—"

"I get it." It hadn't been seventy-two hours since Malcolm disappeared, someone attempted to gain access via the gate, and work began on revamping the security. My guess was there were at least three hundred acres of vineyards, which would be impossible to secure beyond the perimeter. As far as inside the house, nothing would be monitored without Eberly agreeing to it.

"Can I see it?" she asked.

"Of course." When Snapper pulled out his phone and stood, I held my hand out. Instead of showing her himself, he pulled up the footage, then handed his cell to me. I sat beside Eberly and played the video.

"It's hard to tell, but it could be Tiernan," she said, looking up at me.

"Did Vader's guys dust for prints?"

"No luck. Whoever it was, was prepared."

"When did you plan to inform me of this?" I asked, unable to hold the question in any longer.

"He was waiting for my go-ahead." Decker walked into the room from the same direction we'd come in. "You must be Eberly," he said, introducing himself before turning to me. "I need a word. We'll be right back."

I followed him back out to the patio.

"I understand your irritation at not being read in. However, your main job right now is helping Eberly navigate all this shit. There's a crew responsible for security, and you aren't part of it. Am I making myself clear?"

"Perfectly. However, had I known, I wouldn't have brought Eberly here this morning."

He stroked his beard and didn't speak for several seconds. "Fair enough."

I didn't know Decker well and had only interacted with him a few times. However, he didn't strike me as the kind of guy who would admit when he was wrong. Not that he did much beyond conceding I'd made a fair point.

"Eberly thinks it was Tiernan Burke."

"I agree. What I want to know now is what he was doing here. If he was looking for something, best guess is he found it, given how quickly he left. Let's see if Eberly notices anything missing."

We returned to the living room, but neither she nor Snapper were still there. Seconds later, I heard her voice from the other side of the house.

"Who would do this?" she shouted.

I raced over and saw her standing by a set of French doors. Through the window, I could see that what had once been a small garden, maybe no more than ten-by-ten feet, was destroyed. Pots were broken, plants ripped from the ground, and a bench was lying in pieces.

I stood beside her, and she turned to face me. "Enough!" she shouted. "I don't care what any of you think I should or shouldn't do. I'm calling Tiernan today. I'll find out what he wants in order to leave me and my family alone. If it's money, he can have it. All I want is for my father to come home and to live my life in peace."

I understood Eberly's anger and even her desire to "settle" with Burke. My fear was that he'd demand every last cent she had. Particularly if she conveyed the same message to him, which essentially was, "I don't care what it costs."

When my cell rang with a call from Zin, I excused myself and answered. "What's up?" I asked.

"The bank found the missing page from the loan documents. Their attorney is requesting an immediate hearing so they can proceed with the foreclosure."

"What about the Intent to Cure?"

"If they're able to get in front of the judge, he'll insist they issue it regardless. Once they have, the fifteen-day countdown commences. As soon as I receive a response from the courts, I'll let you know. But be prepared. Eberly will need to appear."

"Gotcha," I said before ending the call, hesitating before rejoining the others. Part of me hoped Decker had already convinced Eberly that contacting Burke would be a mistake. Whether he had or not, her plan to confront him would have no impact on Zin's call. The bank's intent to foreclose was an issue on its own, one her former fiancé had no influence over.

As I approached where they stood, my footfalls got heavier in the same way they did when I had to walk past the room where I was attacked. I wished it was in my power to make the shit she was dealing with go away. Then, instead of having to show up for another hearing where she'd once again be slapped in the face with her father's betrayal, we could return to Poppy Hill Ranch and divide our time between mind-blowing sex and planting gardens, both of which put a smile on my little dove's face.

"That was Zin," I began when she, along with Decker and Snapper, turned to face me. I explained what he'd told me about the bank requesting the second hearing after locating the missing page from the loan documents. Like me, Eberly asked about the Intent to Cure, and I passed on Zin's response.

"I'd like to clean this up now if that's okay," she said, motioning outside the door.

My eyes met Decker's, and when he raised a brow, I told him to go ahead.

"Bit mentioned you identified the person in the surveillance footage as Tiernan Burke," he said.

"I said it could be him," she responded. "I'm not certain, though."

"I have a strong suspicion you're right. Based on what we saw, he was in and out of the house in approximately ten minutes. That indicates he may have been looking for something that he was able to locate quickly. I'd like to ask you to look around and see if anything stands out as being missing."

"I already know." She walked toward her father's study, and we followed. "While I don't have a list or a recollection of the contents of the safe, whatever it was must've been in it," she said, pointing to its open door.

When I stepped closer, I saw it was empty.

"Would there have been cash or other things of value? Maybe jewelry?" Decker asked.

"I wouldn't know for sure, but I doubt it."

"Any other ideas?" I asked.

She looked at me with wide eyes. "My trust documents."

"That's probably what it was," said Decker, pulling out his phone. "I'm trying to track the sonuvabitch, but he's a wily fucker," he added under his breath. "Surest sign of an experienced criminal."

If that was what Burke got his hands on, it would mean he'd know Michael Oliver was the trustee. Both him and Zin needed to be updated on that development.

23
Eberly

Trevino insisted he and Snapper pick up the pieces of shattered pottery in the garden, but I ignored them. I wasn't a princess who was afraid of a cut or getting my hands dirty.

No doubt, that's how Tiernan saw me. As someone easy to trample over while he did whatever he wanted, including robbing our family blind. I'd meant it when I said if it was my money he wanted, he could have it. Or at least, that's what I'd make him believe. Once I knew my father was safe, Decker and the *caballeros*, as Trevino referred to them, could tear the man to shreds. I meant that both literally and metaphorically.

When we saw him in Cambria, I would've clawed his eyes out if I knew then what I knew now. Remembering how naive I'd been in the months I dated him made me so angry that I hurled a piece of broken pot at the garden wall, then fell back on my haunches.

"Give us a minute," Trevino said to his brother, who stood and went inside.

"Before you say anything, I feel like an idiot, okay? I don't care about your rule about me disparaging myself. If I'd paid the slightest bit of attention to my own fucking life, I could have prevented all of this."

"Come with me," he said, holding out his hand.

"If you think for one second that you're going to punish me—" I stopped talking when he bent down, picked me up, and carried me through the garden's door. Once we were several yards beyond it, he set me on my feet, then led me over to a sloping hillside that looked out over the vineyard.

"I have no intention of punishing you, nor will I speak to you as disrespectfully as you're speaking to me," he said after we'd both taken a seat on the grass.

I rolled my eyes and shook my head. "This is my life. I've made mistakes, but I don't intend to repeat them. Tiernan tried to control me, and I let him. I won't let you do the same thing."

The look on his face made me wish I could rescind every word. "I didn't mean that," I muttered instead.

"You did mean it, Eberly. Maybe not in the way you think I took it, and that's what I'll address. The difference between Burke and me is that I have no desire to control your life. Not now and not in the future. When we talk about control as it relates to sex, I'll limit what I say to this because I don't want us to get sidetracked rather than focus on what's most important in this conversation. Within a scene, the ultimate control is yours."

I felt my cheeks flush, and as much as I wanted to rail back at him for his admonishment, he wasn't the person I was most angry with. That would be me.

He took my hand and stroked it with his thumb. "I want you to say whatever is on your mind, Eberly, without fear of reprisals from me. I'll ask that you be respectful, but beyond that, the best way I can support you right now is to be your person."

"My person. I don't think I've ever had one of those."

"I bet your mom was. Maybe your dad too, although that may be harder to remember, given current circumstances."

"I'm sorry, Trevino."

"For?"

"Not speaking to you with respect."

"You're forgiven. Now, let's talk about what you said earlier. About contacting Burke."

I looked out at the vineyards. "I want to know my dad is okay. All of this"—I waved my hands—"is stuff. Possessions."

"It's your home."

I looked over at the place where I grew up. "It isn't my house. I have a room in it. Would you live in your mother's house again?"

"Doubtful."

"I don't know why I even care except that it's been in my family for so long. Maybe one of my uncles or my cousins would've wanted it. Not that it's an option any longer."

"It may still be. We haven't seen what the bank found. It could prove inconclusive."

Trevino's cell rang, and he dug it out of his pocket. "It's Zin."

"Go ahead."

"Right, we'll be there as soon as we can," I heard Trevino say before ending the call. "The judge granted the hearing. Zin wants us to meet him at the courthouse."

I had no idea what to expect. I'd already seen the page with my signature and knew it wasn't mine. What purpose did it serve to see the notary's stamp? I could look whoever it was in the face and tell her I'd never seen him or her before, but it would be their word against mine. "I don't know why I need to be there. Or you, for that matter."

"I can't answer that, but Zin can."

I shook my head. "Let's go."

Trevino was quiet on the drive into downtown Paso Robles, more like he used to be when I first started working for him. Before the auction. Before my life fell apart.

My uncle was waiting for us when we walked into the courthouse. "Zin should be here shortly. He's speaking with the bank's counsel now."

"What's going to happen today?" I asked.

"They'll present evidence in order to prove the loan documents are valid. Zin may put you on the stand to testify your signature was forged and that you were unaware the loan existed."

"My word against theirs," I muttered.

"Under oath," my uncle reminded me.

"Let's get this over with," said Zin, walking up from behind us. "I think they're bluffing."

Within minutes of following him in and taking a seat, the judge arrived and the hearing began. I half listened until I heard the other lawyer say they were calling their first witness.

I gasped when I saw the woman I hadn't noticed until now approach the witness box.

"What is she doing here?" I leaned into Trevino and whispered.

"Who?" he asked.

"State your name for the court," said the clerk.

"Nancy Burke."

"What the hell?" Trevino whispered.

"Do you solemnly swear or affirm that the testimony you are about to give will be the truth, the whole truth and nothing but the truth, so help you God?" the clerk asked.

"I do."

When the clerk told her she could be seated, Nancy looked directly at me, then at the lawyer who approached.

My eyes were laser-focused on the woman on the stand as I half listened to the attorney verify she had witnessed the signing of the document that he'd presented as evidence. Before she could respond, Zin objected.

"On what grounds?" the judge asked.

"I wasn't given a copy of whatever evidence is being presented now, nor was I informed of this witness."

"I'll allow it for now, counselor," the judge responded before turning to the other attorney. "Do you have an additional copy?"

"Yes, your honor," he said, walking it over to Zin.

When he reiterated his objection to the witness, the judge overruled him.

"Did you witness the signing of the loan document?" the other lawyer asked.

"I did."

"Are the individuals whose signatures you witnessed in the courtroom today?"

"One is," she responded.

"Can you point to that individual?"

Nancy raised her head and finger. "Her."

"For the record, who is that?"

"Eberly Warwick."

"She's lying!" I shouted, jumping to my feet. "She's lying!" I repeated. "I wasn't there."

My uncle, who was seated at the table with Zin, turned to me when the judge banged his gavel and called for order.

"Eberly, take your seat. We'll handle this."

"Judge, I have to object again." Zin's tone was harsh.

"Approach the bench." He turned to the other lawyer. "You too."

My entire body shook as Nancy was dismissed from the witness box after being told she was excused. I stared at her as she reentered the gallery, but instead of taking a seat, she walked out of the courtroom. Not once did she look at me. I was about to stand to follow her when Trevino put his hand on my arm. "I'll go."

"Let him," said my uncle.

A few seconds later, I heard the judge adjourn the hearing for fifteen minutes. "In my chambers, now," he barked at Zin and the other lawyer as he left the bench.

"What's happening?" I asked my uncle when he turned to face me.

"My guess is that my son is asking the witness' testimony be tossed since he wasn't given prior knowledge of her appearance."

"Mr. Oliver? Ms. Warwick?" a man in a uniform said when he entered the courtroom.

"I'm Mr. Oliver," my uncle responded.

"The judge wants the two of you to join them in the chambers."

"Who is that?" I asked when Uncle Michael motioned for me to follow him.

"The bailiff."

"He isn't the same one who was in here earlier," I whispered as he led us through a door. By the time my uncle realized I was right, it was too late.

24
Bit

I followed Nancy as she raced out of the courthouse and into a vehicle waiting right outside. She made it down the same steps and into the car before I had the chance to see the driver. As it sped off, I took several photos, including a close-up of the license plate.

Knowing there was no way I could get to my truck in time to follow them, I returned inside.

"What the fuck?" I muttered when I entered the courtroom and found it was empty. I was about to call Eberly when the clerk returned from the back.

"Where is everyone?" I asked.

"The attorneys are still in with the judge."

"What about the woman who was seated here earlier?" I motioned to where Eberly and I had been sitting.

"No idea. Maybe she left."

I'd placed the call when the door opened again and Zin walked in, followed by the other attorney and the judge. His brow was furrowed when he approached me.

"Hang on," I said as I listened to her cell ringing endlessly.

"Do these belong to someone?" asked the bailiff, walking through the same door and holding up two cell phones, one of which was ringing.

"Fuck," I said loud enough that the judge raised his head and watched as I ran toward the door, where I was stopped by the same man who held the phones.

Zin rushed over to the bench. "The phones you have belong to my father and Ms. Warwick," he hurriedly explained. While the attention was focused on him, I raced around the bailiff and through the door.

"Eberly? Michael?" I shouted as I continued running.

"Sir, you can't be in here," I heard someone shout from behind me.

"Where's the exit?" I yelled just as another man jumped in front of me, blocking my way.

"Let him go!" I heard Zin yell, racing in my direction. "This way," he motioned as he ran past me.

He opened a door leading to an underground parking structure, and we both went in opposite directions.

"I'll call Vader, you call your brother," Zin shouted behind him when he went to the right and I went left.

As I frantically searched for any sign of them, I called Snapper. "Eberly and Michael are gone," I shouted into the phone. "We're at the courthouse."

"Nothing?" Zin asked when we met on the opposite side.

I shook my head.

"What the fuck happened?" he yelled, spinning in a circle.

"Tiernan," I said.

He turned to face me. "He's got them."

Decker Ashford set up a command center in Zin's office and started barking orders at everyone but me.

"Give me something to do," I practically begged, stepping in front of him.

"Start canvassing businesses in the surrounding area for CCTV footage." He turned to Snapper. "You go with him."

We reached the elevator at the same time Kick stepped off with Cru. "Addy's in labor. Brix is with her at the hospital. Ridge, Press, and Bones are on their way. What can we do?"

"Talk to Decker," Snapper told him, motioning to Zin's office as I pushed past them and repeatedly jabbed the elevator button once I was on it. He jumped on with me right before the door closed.

"How are you doin', Bit?"

"How do you think?" I snarled.

"We're gonna find her. Decker's calling the cavalry in from all over."

I didn't know what that meant, and I didn't care. I had no doubt Tiernan Burke—or whoever the fuck he was—was behind this, and God knew where he took her and Michael Oliver.

"I'll kill him with my bare hands," I seethed.

I was partway down the second block from the courthouse when I received an urgent group text from Decker, telling everyone to return to Zin's office.

I ran back, arriving at the building at the same time a car pulled up and Tryst jumped out. When he followed me in and onto the elevator, I faced the wall and put my head in my hands as I tried to catch my breath more from an impending panic attack than the run.

Tryst grabbed my arms and spun me around to face him. "You cannot fall apart now, Trevino. Eberly needs you to remain in control. She needs you to find her."

My eyes darted between his.

His fingers dug into my flesh. "You can do this. Eberly needs you to do this."

I nodded. "Yes. She's mine."

He nodded too. "She's yours to protect, Bit. It is your responsibility, your pledge to her."

"Yes," I repeated.

Tryst moved his hand to my neck. "Ready?"

The elevator door opened, and I squared my shoulders. "Ready."

"Have a seat so we can get through this as fast as possible," Decker said when we came inside.

"I'm good."

He leveled a glare at me, and I sat, watching the screen as Burke's photo appeared.

"Gentlemen, this is Liam Devaney, aka Tiernan Burke, grandson of Christopher Devaney, who is the founder of the gang of the same name. The Devaney organization is considered to be Ireland's most powerful crime family. Liam, it seems, was tapped to take over what the Killeens and FAIM left behind after last year's raid. Either that, or he took it upon himself to go after the combined territories, either with or without permission from his granddaddy. I'll wager it's without, which is why he's gotta build a stockpile of cash."

Another photo appeared beside it. "As you can see, his appearance has been altered since the photo on the right was taken three years ago."

I had to agree, while the man in the two images appeared to be the same height and weight, otherwise, they looked drastically different. The most remarkable thing about him, his eye color, wasn't discernible, given the lighting of both photos.

"At the time the second image was taken, Liam landed on several countries' most wanted lists, including the FBI's and the NCA's—the UK's National Crime Agency. The two agencies put up a reward money amounting to five million dollars each for his capture as well as the same for Christopher Devaney, Senior and Junior, Miranda and Patrick Boyle, and James Dunn."

Two more images appeared on the screen. There was enough of a resemblance for the woman to be Nancy Burke or someone related to her.

"Is Devaney connected to Grogan?" I asked.

"Affirmative," Decker responded. "After we've located Eberly Warwick, her father, and Michael Oliver, we'll do a complete briefing on how."

Three more men dressed in tactical gear walked into the conference room where we were gathered. "This is Sebastian Steel, Bronson Dunning, and Mick Reynolds. Each is among the world's best in critical-incident response and hostage rescue. What that means is their teams are gonna find the motherfuckers who have 'em and we're gonna bring 'em home."

Decker's eyes met mine, and I nodded.

"We've been able to bring in some extra firepower from one of our friends at the NRO. His code name is Grit. You got anything for us yet, buddy?"

"Affirmative, and it's good news, boys. I've got a twenty for you," said a guy Decker had on speakerphone.

"Bit, you're with me. Tryst, you too. Everyone else was assigned before you got here." Decker said when a satellite image appeared on the screen. "Let's move out."

25
Eberly

Once we walked through the door leading to the judge's chambers, two other men met us, both with guns. Unlike the "bailiff," they wore masks to cover their faces. Our hands were tied behind us, and we were pulled as much as led down a corridor and out into a parking structure, where we were shoved into a waiting vehicle with blackened windows. Had my wrists not been bound, I would've lunged at the driver—Nancy. When her eyes met mine, I saw the same hatred I felt for her reflected back at me.

A hood was put over my head, and I was pushed down on the floorboards. No doubt, they did the same to Uncle Michael.

We drove for a while—maybe twenty minutes—in town, based on the number of times we stopped and waited the length of a signal change. Then they got on a highway. Again, we traveled maybe twenty or thirty minutes before exiting. After several turns, the vehicle stopped and the engine turned off. Doors opened, and

I was pulled out, but without enough time to get to my feet, I fell onto the pavement.

"Get her inside, you *feckin' eegit*," a woman who sounded like Nancy said, except now with a distinct Irish accent. It was the first I'd heard any of them speak.

The way my knee stung, I knew I'd scraped it, but my captor's rough handling hurt equally bad.

"Eberly—" my uncle began.

"No talking," another voice said, also with an Irish accent.

We were led outside over uneven grass and dirt, then into what I knew were caves, based on the immediate and significant drop in temperature. The all-too-familiar smell of barrels storing wine confirmed my suspicions that we'd been taken to a vineyard.

After the captor lowered me into a chair, he bound me to it, then removed the hood. "Dad?" I gasped.

His face was ashen, and his eyes were bloodshot as though he'd been crying, and like me, he was bound to a chair. He shook his head slightly, glanced in the direction of the masked man tying my uncle up, then lowered his head.

Once he went upstairs and we heard the door close, my father looked up. "I'm so sorry," he said, his voice strained and barely above a whisper. "Both of you."

"Is it safe to talk?" my uncle asked, also in a low tone of voice.

My father smiled as much as sneered. "Based on everything I've said, every name I've called Burke, I doubt I'd still be alive if they were listening in."

"Dad, what happened?"

He lowered his head again, and I could see he was crying.

"It's okay. We don't have to talk about it."

He raised his head again and looked from me to Uncle Michael. "We need to."

"Okay," I whispered, waiting for him to begin.

"You'd been dating Burke for a few months when he and I met up in the winery. I thought it was random, but now I realize nothing was with him. Not even meeting you." He brushed his face on his shoulder and took a deep breath. "From that day on, he carefully pieced together the plan that landed us in this room."

"He forced you to sell the winery?" my uncle asked.

"At first, I thought he was trying to help me save it. You know, for Eberly. He was aware enough to know that we were in trouble, like so many of us were after the pandemic and subsequent saturation of the market. I told him too much that day."

"Is that when he suggested selling to the consortium?" I asked.

"He offered it as one option, but given the other choices, that made the most sense. When I told him I needed to discuss it with you first, that was the day my life descended into hell."

I listened as he struggled to tell me how Tiernan had threatened my life if my dad didn't go along with his demands.

"By that point, you were engaged, and as much as I wanted to come clean, I couldn't. Burke made it clear, in no uncertain terms, that if I did…" He cried openly so hard that his body shook. "He's not who he says he is," he was finally able to say. "He's connected to organized crime, one of the most powerful criminal enterprises in the world."

"The Irish mob?" Uncle Michael asked.

"Yes, and Burke is not his real name, although he hasn't let on what it is."

"That's the reason you didn't involve law enforcement," my uncle added.

"I couldn't risk it."

"Understood."

My dad turned to me. "After forging your signature on the winery sale, he forced me to mortgage the house. Nancy works for him, along with the goons who abducted the two of you."

"Earlier today, she testified that I signed the paperwork."

"Burke used her to keep me in line when he wasn't around to do it himself."

"He said you were the one to call off the wedding."

"I was—in a way. All along, he believed that, by marrying you, he'd be able to get his hands on your trust fund. When I told him he wouldn't through marriage, that it was stated within the terms of the fiduciary fund and that it was irrevocable, he went along with ending the engagement."

"Why did he give up so easily?"

"I thought the same thing, but quickly realized he hadn't."

"Is that the day you left?"

"It was. He intended to kidnap you, Eberly, and demand the full amount of the trust as ransom. Once he had the money, I knew he'd kill us both. I decided to strike first." He broke down again. "I failed."

"He figured out I was the trustee," Uncle Michael said more than asked.

"Yes, and I anticipate that, any minute now, he'll demand you liquidate the trust and have the money in it wired to an offshore account."

"That will not be instantaneous, given the amount of assets that will have to be converted."

My father nodded, and for the first time, I saw a familiar glimmer in his eyes. That was what he was counting on, as was I.

26
Bit

It made sense that the place where Devaney took Eberly and Michael was a defunct winery that had been part of the consortium and that was subsequently dismantled.

Based on the overheads, as Decker called them, they were taken into wine caves similar to the ones at Los Cab, but far smaller.

Wine caves. As soon as he'd said the words, I felt Tryst's eyes on me. Instead of looking at him, I turned my head toward the car window. I was okay, and I'd be okay, and as long as I was sure of it, I didn't need him to be. Where we were headed was about rescuing Eberly and getting her out of the clutches of a man I hoped would draw his last breath today—if not by someone else's hand, then by mine. All I knew for certain was that he wouldn't be taken alive.

"Once we arrive, we'll use a Doppler device to determine where they're being held," Decker, who'd changed into tactical gear before we left, said over his shoulder. He was seated in the front passenger seat; Snapper was driving. "According to what I can see from the imagery the NRO provided, there is a second way in and out of the caves." He held a tablet near the center console so Tryst and I could see it. "We'll enter the property over these hills." He pointed at the screen. "Then I'll go in with Steel and his team from the front. Vex, Jagger, and their crews will go in the other way."

He handed me a comms device. "You are to remain outside the caves until you hear me specifically tell you to enter. Any disregard of my direct order may result in loss of life, and when I say that, I'm talking about Eberly, Michael, and Malcolm. Are we clear?"

"Yes, sir."

"Do we know for certain this is where Malcolm is being held as well?" Tryst asked.

"We do not. However, confirming it won't be difficult once we arrive."

"How much farther?" I asked.

"Fifteen minutes," Snapper responded.

"How is Devaney connected to Grogan?" I pressed.

"Half brothers," Deck responded. "One turned out to be what we presume is the heir apparent."

"The other is a meth-head," I muttered.

"I haven't been able to figure out when he was shipped off to America. I do know he was born in Ireland."

"It doesn't matter," I said under my breath.

"No, it doesn't, Bit. However, your actions the night of the auction are what led me to delve deeper into Devaney's real identity. I would've gotten there eventually; thanks to you, it happened quicker."

"I should've killed him that night. I might've if I'd found him."

"This way will be a lot cleaner, and you won't end up in prison for murder."

I raised my head and met his gaze.

"Got it?"

"If you mean let someone else handle it, I can't make any promises."

His phone vibrated. "Well, I'll be damned."

"What happened?"

"While searching for Liam, I stumbled on a possible lead on his father's and grandfather's whereabouts. Both were apprehended earlier today. One in Spain, and the other in Dubai."

"Well done, Decker," said Tryst.

The man shrugged a shoulder. "All part of the job."

I shut my eyes and rested my head against the seat, attempting to clear my head and shut off the noise. I clenched my fists against the overwhelming itch I felt to leave the minute I knew Eberly was safe.

It was my fault she'd been kidnapped, in the first place. I never should've left her, especially for as long as I had. I was supposed to keep her safe, and I hadn't. How could she ever trust me again?

When I felt the telltale signs of a migraine coming on, I rubbed my left temple.

"Trevino?" Tryst said, resting his hand on my arm.

"I'll be okay."

When he put his hand on the back of my neck, then pressed his thumbs on either side of the base of my skull, I didn't jerk away. It was Tryst who'd taught me about the pressure points referred to as the gates of consciousness. There were others he'd shown me, but this one was the quickest I'd found to alleviate the pressure that could become debilitating.

The first time Eberly was in my bed, she'd done the same thing, and I'd slept. The love I felt for her was more than I realized was possible. If anything happened to her…

"Breathe deeply, Trevino," Tryst whispered. "Eberly needs you."

Since my eyes were closed, I had no idea whether Decker had noticed what was happening. Most likely, he did, given he didn't miss much. Except I didn't care whether he saw or what he thought. Pride couldn't stand in my way when the debilitating pain I so often experienced might prevent me from being there when the love of my life needed me the most. I'd failed her once. I wouldn't again.

I raised my head and opened my eyes.

"Better?"

"I think so."

"This is it," said Decker, motioning to a fire road.

Snapper pulled off at the same time I heard one of the other guys say through the comms that they were in position.

"ETA two minutes," Decker responded.

Snapper pulled right behind an outcropping of trees. Not far from where he parked, I could see one man, but not any of the others.

I closed my eyes and listened after Decked exited the vehicle. Once he was in position, he signaled the others to enter the caves. I could hear the sound of boots on the ground, but nothing else.

Then my blood froze.

"Let her go, and toss your weapon this way," I heard Decker say. "You're surrounded, and there's no way out alive unless you do."

"Clear out of my way, or she gets a bullet in her brain. As soon as she does, the other two will too." While the voice sounded like Burke's, the accent was Irish.

I was out of the vehicle before Tryst or Snapper could stop me, headed for something else I saw from where we parked—another way into the caves.

Three steps led down to an entrance obscured by overgrowth, similar to the one we had leading into the old winery. Ours went to a secret passageway my father thought his father had used during prohibition. Rather than connecting to the main corridor, ours went behind the storage rooms. I had no doubt these did too.

Knowing I'd find them easier by listening to voices echoing on the stone, I reached up and turned the comms down enough that I could still hear it, but faintly. At the same time, I readied my gun, eased the wooden door open, and raced inside what looked more like a tunnel than a corridor.

It only led in one direction, and since I couldn't see a fucking thing, I hugged the wall and ran.

When the voices got closer, I slowed, tuning out the words and focusing solely on feeling my way. I hadn't found an offshoot yet, but there had to be something leading into the storage rooms.

"I've got him," I heard someone say through the comms, not realizing he was talking about me until I heard Decker say, "Typical Bit."

"I can't find a way in," I responded.

"Two more feet on the left," said the first guy. It didn't make sense since the sounds I could hear were on the right, but I went in that direction anyway.

I jolted when I heard the sound of gunfire farther in the distance.

"If you want to live, drop the gun, Devaney. We already took your buddies out."

"You shoot me, and Eberly dies."

"So, what are you thinkin', asshole? You've got four snipers with their guns aimed right between your eyes. You think you're somehow gonna make it outta here?

Give it up. You're done in the same way your father and grandfather are."

"Another foot, and you'll round a bend. It'll put you right behind him. Deck, you ready?"

I came around in time to see Decker take a step forward and the man move the gun away from Eberly's temple. The split second the distraction allowed gave me my one chance to take him out. I fired first. Two more came after.

Eberly screamed when I grabbed her around the waist and pulled her into the tunnel.

"Shh, I've got you, little dove," I said, pulling the comms device out of my ear.

"Trevino?"

"Did you think I wouldn't come?" I asked, not giving her the chance to respond before kissing her.

"I knew you would," she said when I broke the kiss.

"Come on. Let's get out of here."

"I can't see anything."

"You don't need to. Follow my lead, in the same way you would if we were dancing." I squeezed her hand, and she squeezed back. We'd gone another foot or two when I saw light shining ahead of us.

"This way," said Tryst, who I could now see clearly.

"What about my dad and Uncle Michael?" she asked.

"They're waiting right outside," my uncle reassured her.

I led her up the three steps, but when I tried to release her hand, she held tight. "Don't let me go yet," she said, turning in my arms once we were above ground.

"Never, little dove."

27

Eberly

"There will be time to talk later. For now, let's get out of the way and let the cleanup crew do their job," said Decker, motioning to two waiting SUVs.

"Wait," I said when Trevino released me. I closed the distance between my father and me, and when he opened his arms, we embraced.

"I'm so sorry for everything," he said. "The winery, the house, the lies."

I rested my head on his chest. "It was to protect me, Dad. You saved my life." I couldn't tell him now how I hadn't given him the benefit of the doubt or that I'd believed he'd willingly defrauded me out of my home. I owed it to him, though. He deserved my apology more than I did his.

"What about Nancy?" I asked when my father released me and we were walking toward one of the SUVs.

"Dead. They all are," said Decker. "I'd like to do a hotwash, err, after-incident brief now, if you're feeling up to it."

"Of course," I said when my father and uncle said they were.

"We can return to Los Caballeros if that—"

"I'd prefer to go home," said my dad.

"Of course," Decker responded.

Trevino held my hand, then helped me into the SUV. "Aren't you coming with us?" I asked when he didn't get in after I slid to the middle.

"I thought you'd rather ride with your dad and uncle."

"Of course I would, but I want to be with you more."

When he climbed in beside me, there was a tightness to his eyes. I'd ask what was wrong, but he wouldn't want me to as long as we had an audience. I put my arm through his and rested my head on his shoulder. Rather than relax into me, his muscles remained taut. I was about to pull away, but Trevino held me tight to his side. We'd talk later, once we were alone, I reminded myself.

My father sat on the other side of me, and Uncle Michael got in the front passenger seat.

"Ready?" Trevino's brother Snapper asked.

Even though no one answered, he put the truck in reverse and drove down a gravel road.

"What winery is this?" my uncle asked.

"It was Hope Springs," said Snapper.

"Also taken out by the consortium," my father muttered. "It was in Lucas Hope's family for decades."

"He's Saffron and Felicity's father, right?" I asked.

"Yes," Snapper answered before my dad. I could see his grip on the steering wheel tighten.

A half hour later, when we pulled up to the newly installed gate of our estate, my father's eyes widened, but he didn't say anything.

"I'll go over the new security systems later," Snapper said over his shoulder.

My dad didn't respond, but when I put my free hand in his, he looked at me and squeezed it.

I could only imagine the guilt he must feel, but like I'd said before we got on the road, everything he did was to protect me.

Could that be the cause of the tension I felt from Trevino too? Did he believe he'd somehow failed me?

Snapper pulled up near the front door to let us out. Trevino went ahead of me to enter his code to open it.

Once inside, my father looked around as if it had been far longer than a few days since he'd been here. Apart from the secret garden being destroyed, nothing had changed.

He stood in the entryway, and his eyes filled with tears. "It's okay, Dad. We'll figure this out together."

There was a knock at the door. Trevino opened it, and Decker, Zin, and Kick came inside.

"Let's go in here," I said, motioning to the living room. "Can I get anyone anything?"

"I'll take care of it. You sit down," Trevino said.

Snapper put his hand on his brother's arm. "Let me, Bit."

We sat on the sofa like we did in the SUV. Trevino on one side of me, and my dad on the other.

"I'm going to start with what we learned about Tiernan Burke and the others responsible for the abduction," said Decker. "Prior to your rescue, we learned Burke's real identity. He was Liam Devaney, grandson of Christopher Devaney. Who, along with Liam's father, was arrested earlier today."

My father stiffened, and I put my hand on his.

"What we believe is that after the raid and dismantling of both the Killeens and FAIM a year ago, the Devaneys saw an opportunity to take over their territories here in the States. We also believe the intention was to build a war chest, if you will, of cash." He looked at Trevino, then at me, then my dad. "While it was buried under the guise of an LLC, the crime syndicate held controlling interest in the Wine Consortium. Not that it changes anything, but the Warwick family was just one of those targeted. You should also know that, once it went public, it appears the Devaneys dumped their shares of stock, resulting in a big payday. Although insider trading would be the least of their crimes at this point."

"How was Nancy Burke involved?" I asked. "I mean, I know she was the notary who testified I'd signed the loan documents."

"Her real identity is Miranda Boyle, Liam's sister. She, along with her husband, Patrick, and a man named James Dunn, were the three others killed along with Devaney."

My father took a deep breath and hung his head.

"Malcolm?"

He looked up at Decker.

"When you're ready, we'll want to take a statement about the chain of events that led up to your kidnapping. That isn't something we need to do today. In fact, it would be best to wait for the sheriff."

"He just pulled in," Trevino said, looking beyond me and out the window.

"In that case, we can do it now," said my father.

Decker studied him. "If you're sure."

"I am. I'd rather get this over with and start working to clean up the mess I've made of our lives."

Trevino's silence worried me, and since I'd already heard my father's side of the story, I asked Decker if they needed me for this part.

"Not necessarily," he responded.

"Can you come with me?" I asked Trevino.

He nodded and stood when I did.

"Mind if we go outside?" I asked.

"That's fine," he muttered.

I led him to the same bench where we'd sat when I told him about my mother and I working together on the butterfly garden. "Talk to me," I said once we were seated.

He leaned forward and rested his elbows on his knees.

"Please, Trevino."

He glanced over at me, and I saw his eyes fill with tears. Rather than speak, he shook his head.

"Okay, I will, then."

He turned his head and looked out at the vineyards.

"Because of you—and my dad—I'm alive. My father protected me from Tiernan, err, Liam, then you did too."

"I failed you," he said, barely above a whisper.

"Look at me."

He sat up straight.

"You saved my life."

"If it weren't for me, you wouldn't have been in danger in the first place."

My eyes bored into his. "I disagree. If you'd been in the courtroom when the bailiff told my uncle and me that the judge wanted to see us in his chambers, you would've been abducted too."

"Is that what happened?"

I told him how, as soon as we were through the door leading out of the courtroom, I realized the man who'd asked us to follow him wasn't the same one I'd seen a few minutes earlier. And that, by the time my uncle and I realized it, it was too late.

Trevino looked up at the sky. "I'll never forgive myself—"

"Stop this."

His eyes opened wide at my response. "Eberly, I—"

"No. I won't allow you to do this. You are in no way to blame for anything that's happened. All you've done since the moment I met you was care for me, care about me, in a way no one other than my parents ever has. You know me better than anyone, even them, so you also know that it's because of you that the way I'm speaking to you right now isn't something I would've been able to do a month ago."

I saw a half smile. "You would've. Just like the day at the old winery when you told me what was what."

"Do you mean the Stonehouse and Gardens?"

He chuckled. "Yeah, the day you renamed the place."

"That was still because of you, Trevino. I knew then that I could trust you enough to speak my mind, something I'd rarely ever done. I knew you'd listen and not make me feel stupid for sharing my ideas."

"I hate that you felt anyone would make you feel stupid, little dove."

I smiled, and my eyes filled with tears.

"What?" he asked.

"I love it when you call me that. I've been waiting for you to since we left Hope Springs." I wove my fingers with his. "There's something I need from you."

"Anything."

"Be you, Trevino. Be the guy who tells me there will be consequences if I say something bad about myself. Be the guy I feel safe with, protected by, loved by. Stop thinking you didn't do everything you could to save my life."

He grinned. "And if I don't?"

I pursed my lips and scrunched my eyes. "Then, *you'll* face consequences."

"Come here," he said, pulling me onto his lap. "I love you, little dove."

I wriggled when I felt his hardness pressed against me. "Even when I get mad at you?"

"Especially when you do."

I raised a brow. "Is that right?"

He reached under me and squeezed my bottom. "I'm thinking of ways I can punish you."

My cheeks flushed, and my pussy clenched. "So am I, sir."

28

Bit
Two weeks later

"How's it going?" Brix asked when he walked into the Stonehouse, as I now called it, with his wife and their baby.

"Almost ready," I said, climbing down from the ladder where I was replacing a bulb in the strung lights. I walked over to the stroller and knelt down. "She's gotten so big," I said, reaching out to stroke the baby's cheek with my fingertip.

"Reagan is going to miss her Uncle Bit," said Addison.

"You don't have to return to Mexico, you know."

They'd been in town since little Reagan was born but had announced, the night before, they were leaving for their ranch in Alamos, which was adjacent to Tryst's.

"Uh-oh, somebody's hungry," said Addy when the baby started to cry. She leaned up and kissed Brix's cheek. "I'm going to take her to the cottage. We'll see you later."

Since Cru and Daphne were living in the house that used to belong to Brix, and Eberly and I were spending most of our time at Poppy Hill, the cottage had served as their base while they were in California. No doubt, our mother would've preferred they stay in the main house with her, but I got that Brix and Addy would prefer to be on their own with their daughter.

"I got a call from Decker. He said he's been trying to reach you," said my brother.

"I've been busy getting this place ready for my date with Eberly tonight. I figured I'd return his call in a few days."

"Understood, except I think there's some urgency in what he wants to discuss with you."

I scowled. "Eberly is my priority—"

"It involves her, Bit."

That got my attention. The last few weeks had been hard for her and her father, trying to figure out how to save their house. She was willing to use money from her trust fund to pay off the loan, but her dad, along with the rest of the *caballeros*, was reluctant to allow her to do it, given there was still a case to be made that the loan was fraudulent.

"I'll call him."

"He's on his way here now."

I sighed. "I don't have time for this."

"Sure you do," said Snapper, who'd walked in, in the middle of our conversation. He wasn't alone. Cru, Kick, and Alex were with him.

"Mom's on her way," said my sister. "So are Justine, Saffron, and Felicity. While you guys have your *secret* meeting, the girls and I will finish getting the place ready for tonight."

As hard as it was for me to let them do it, if whatever Decker wanted to talk to me about involved Eberly, I had to hear him, get it over with, then return and finish setting up.

"Look, I know you want everything to be perfect," said Alex, putting her arm through mine. "Once your meeting is over, you can inspect our work and tell us everything we did wrong." She winked.

It dawned on me then that she'd said "secret meeting."

"Is Decker meeting us in the caves?" While that was the way I chose to phrase the question, what I was really asking was if he was being invited to meet with Los Caballeros.

"I spoke with the *viejos*, and they agreed," said Brix. "What he has to tell us affects Malcolm Warwick as well as Lucas Hope."

I glanced over at Alex.

"What? Do you really think I haven't known about Los Caballeros most of my life? I still don't get why you don't have any female members." She huffed.

"*Caballeros*, not *caballeras*," muttered Brix.

Alex rolled her eyes. "Yeah, whatever. Be on your way so Bit can get ready for his big date. Eberly bid a lot of money for it. He owes her." She winked.

What Alex didn't know was that what I'd planned for tonight wasn't as much about my little dove's auction bid as it was the rest of our lives.

Rather than meet where we usually gathered, we set up in one of the larger rooms inside the caves.

"Decker's here," said Brix. "Do you want to meet him outside and bring him in?"

"I can do it," Cru offered.

I shook my head. The more I walked past where I'd been left for dead, the easier it would be each time I had to do it. "I'll be okay." My eyes met Tryst's.

"Yes, you will be, Bit," he said.

"Sorry to waylay you from your big plans tonight," Decker said when I met him at the caves' entrance.

"Yeah, well, make it quick." I scowled and he laughed.

"Typical Bit."

I led him to the room where the rest of the *caballeros* waited.

"So this is the inner sanctum?" he joked, looking around the space that was used for larger wine dinners.

"Nah, we can't allow you in there," said Brix, squeezing his shoulder.

I glanced over to where Eberly's father sat and walked over to take the empty seat beside him. I knew the man was plagued with guilt in the same way I would be in his shoes. I hoped that whatever Decker had to say would be good news in terms of the house, if not the winery.

"Thanks for allowing me an audience," Deck said once we were seated. I didn't hear sarcasm in his words, only respect. "I've come to you to help me determine the best use of the reward money offered for the capture of the Devaneys." Before I could ask what he was talking about, he continued. "As we know, it wasn't only Christopher and his son who were on the FBI's and NCA's most-wanted list. Liam Devaney, Miranda and Patrick Boyle, and James Dunn were too. Each of them had reward money offered for their capture. Five million from the FBI and another five from the NCA. Given it was dead or alive, the total amount the US and UK governments are willing to pay out is over sixty million dollars since part of that is in pounds."

"Why are you asking us?" I spoke out.

"Because if it weren't for you, Bit, they never would've been taken out. They wouldn't have even been on our radar."

"It wasn't me alone."

"No, it wasn't, which is why I'm not suggesting all sixty mil be handed over to you."

Those in the room chuckled. Decker did too, then his expression turned more serious. "I have a proposal I'd like you to consider."

"Go ahead," said Tryst, who was standing near the rear of the room.

"We establish a fund used to purchase the wineries put out of business by the consortium."

The room turned quiet until Malcolm cleared his throat. "While that is very generous, it isn't fair. My winery was failing long before the consortium entered the picture."

"As was mine," said Lucas Hope.

"There were four Central Coast wineries driven out of business by the Wine Consortium," said Tryst, stepping forward and standing next to Decker. "I move we vote to use the reward money to purchase the four wineries and deed them to their original owners."

"Anyone want to second that?" asked Brix.

"Hang on." Malcolm stood. "There were more than four of us. A few small enterprises in Napa were affected as well."

"From what I remember, none of them aided in capturing of the Devaneys," said Decker, who'd turned to face Malcolm. "And while I'm sure everyone in this room appreciates your humility and graciousness, my understanding is there's a motion currently on the floor."

Baron Van Orr stood and turned toward Malcolm. "I second the motion."

"All those in favor?" prompted Brix.

Every hand went up besides Malcolm's and Lucas'.

"Opposed?" Brix continued. No one raised a hand.

"The motion carries by majority vote. The two abstentions are noted."

The meeting was adjourned, and as anxious as I was to return to the Stonehouse, I waited when Malcolm and Lucas approached Decker, Tryst, and Brix.

"I truly don't know what to say," said Malcolm, extending his hand to shake those of all three men. "It doesn't feel right."

"It's what Los Caballeros does," said Tryst. "We help those in need, sometimes without them ever knowing it. Why wouldn't we do the same for our brothers as we would for strangers?"

"I don't mind seein' the government's ponying up for it," said Decker. "Two, in fact."

"You're entitled to that money as much as anyone else is," I said to him.

"Yeah? Well, what the hell am I gonna do with it?"

29
Eberly

Yesterday, Trevino and I took a walk on Moonstone Beach, then went for a motorcycle ride on See Canyon Road. Once we'd returned to the beach, we had a romantic dinner at the Sea Chest. Tonight, he said he'd take me on the last part of the date I'd bid on at the Wicked Winemakers bachelor auction.

I told him he didn't have to do any of it, particularly since he'd paid for my bid, but he insisted. I had to admit I loved that he did.

As hard as the last two weeks—actually three—had been, they were the best of my life. I was sad that the bank was taking our house, my father was refusing to allow me to pay off the loan, and our family's winery was out of business, but the way Trevino felt about me, treated me, loved me, made me realize how insignificant that all was. I'd carry the memories of my mom, dad, and me in my heart forever. They wouldn't be left behind when someone else moved into the house I grew up in. I knew my father would struggle with guilt for a long time, but there wasn't anything more I could do to assuage it. That he was alive was what mattered most to me.

The night after we were rescued, Trevino and I had stayed up until dawn talking about life and love and sex. Actually, having a lot of sex.

We'd finally gone over our list of limits, which I'd insisted on even after he said we could do it another time. When he looked into my eyes and told me he'd be willing to give up the "kinky stuff," as he'd call it, if I wanted him to, I told him in the most honest and direct way I could that I loved it. I loved calling him sir, I loved it when he took control, "forcing" me to endure pleasure like I'd never dreamed of, and I even loved it when he punished me. I'd put his hand between my legs, proving that I needed as much as wanted it.

In the hours and days that followed, I spent more time naked, and loving it, and had more mind-blowing orgasms than I could remember. Each time was better than the last. Each time, my love for him grew deeper.

While I'd spent every night at Poppy Hill Ranch with Trevino, I'd come home to get ready for our date, and a few minutes before he arrived to pick me up, I came downstairs, and my father was waiting at the bottom.

"You look so beautiful, Eb. So much like your mom."

"Thank you," I said, taking his hand when he held it out to me.

"There's something I need to tell you. Do you have a minute?"

I checked the time. "Trevino won't be here for another fifteen at least."

"Good," he said, leading me into the living room. "Something significant happened this afternoon. A group of investors, if you will, are allowing me to save the winery."

"That's fabulous news." I was stunned but also worried. "I hate to be negative, but are you sure you can trust this group?"

"I've never been more certain of anything."

Something occurred to me. "Does this have anything to do with Los Caballeros?"

His eyes widened, then scrunched.

"Not the winery, Dad, the *caballeros*."

"It does, but…"

"How do I know? Trevino told me, and before you ask, he had permission to."

"I see."

"In the same way you were able to tell Mom."

"Tell me one thing," he said, taking my hand in his. "Do you love him?"

"More than I dreamed possible. He's a good man who loves me equally."

"I'm happy for you, Eb. I think your mom would be too."

I shook my head. "I know she would. She told me once that Trevino was her favorite of all the Avila boys. She also said it was because he reminded her of you."

He looked down at our clasped hands. "I'm not sure I deserve that praise."

"Trevino gets upset with me when I say negative things about myself. I understand now why he does."

"What do you mean?"

"It hurts to hear someone you love be down on themselves."

"I'm sorry, Eb, but—"

I shook my head. "I can't hear it anymore. I won't."

His eyes met mine.

"I'm serious. I've forgiven you and I understand why you did it. Now, you need to forgive yourself."

"I'm working on it."

"Work harder." I looked out the window when I saw Trevino's truck pulling through the gate. "He's here."

We both stood and walked to the front door.

"He could've driven something other than that truck. Look at you. You're in a gown and heels—"

"And he's in a tuxedo. Besides, I love that truck. If he'd arrived in anything else, I would've been disappointed."

My father chuckled.

"It's nice to hear you laugh."

"Hello, sir," Trevino said, walking up to the front door. "And wow. You are stunning."

I loved the way he looked me up and down, eyes blazing and a huge smile on his face. It made me feel beautiful and sexy and cherished.

"I was just saying that, as fancy as you're dressed, I'm surprised you drove that old thing."

As much as I wanted to smack my dad, Trevino's response was perfect.

"Eberly loves my old truck. Maybe even more than she loves me."

30
Bit

There was no reason for me to be nervous. I'd never known anyone who soothed me the same way Eberly did. As long as her hand was in mine, as long as she loved me, I knew I'd never feel that itch to leave again.

Tonight, though, I couldn't help but be anxious, mainly because it was important to me that it be perfect.

Snapper gave me the same shit about picking Eberly up in my truck as her dad did, but I knew better. She loved being able to sit right next to me as much as I loved feeling her by my side.

When I'd returned from the Los Caballeros' meeting, Alex had worked her magic, making the Stonehouse look more beautiful than I ever could have.

I'd thanked her and Eberly's friends who'd shown up to help over and over again, as I spun in a circle, taking it in. "She's going to love this," I'd said. "It looks amazing."

My sister had put her arm in mine. "I'll let you in on a secret, Bit. She'd love it if you spread a blanket on the floor and served a picnic, because being with you is what really matters to her." When her eyes filled with tears, she'd punched me. "Go get ready, for God's sake."

Now, here we were. I led her inside, where the lights twinkled, soft music played, and dinner was waiting under domes on the table.

"Would you like a glass of wine?" I asked, letting go of her hand to walk over to the bar.

"Wait," she said, catching my wrist. "You know what I'd really like?"

"Tell me, little dove," I said, cupping her cheek.

"I want to dance with you first."

I spun her around and around the room that was filled with bouquets of her favorite flowers and, at the end of the song, got down on one knee.

My hand shook when I took the small box from my pocket and gazed up at her beautiful face. "Marry me, little dove? Be mine forever?"

Her eyes filled with tears. "Yes, yes, yes, I'll marry you."

She gasped when I slid the ring on her finger. Her father gave it to me the day I'd told him I planned to propose. It was the same ring he'd given to her mother.

"Oh, Trevino. I love it and you so much."

***

The day after we were married, only a week after I proposed, I gave her the other gift her father and I had agreed upon together—her house. I'd purchased it from the bank but had the deed made out in her name.

She fussed at me about it, but I knew it made her happy. Especially when she told me that she'd always dreamed of turning it into a bed and breakfast.

Her dad, who'd already moved into the guesthouse on the property while we were on our honeymoon, ended up taking over its management right after our first baby was born.

We named him Trystan Trevino, but most of the time, Eberly called him her "little bit."

Keep reading for a sneak peek
at the next book in the
Wicked Winemakers Second Label series,
Snapper's Seduction

He's a champion team roper, living a double life as an undercover operative.
She's a vineyard heiress, fighting for respect in her family's wine business.
Their blossoming romance becomes a deadly game when the cartel comes calling.

SNAPPER

I've always lived my life in two worlds: the roar of the rodeo arena and the shadows of covert operations. But when Saffron Hope walked into my life with her vintage wines and fierce determination, everything changed. Now, her best friend is missing, taken by a cartel boss I've been tracking for years, and the woman I'm falling for insists on helping with the rescue, but bringing Saffron into my dangerous world could cost us everything.

SAFFRON

All I wanted was to prove myself worthy of running my family's winery. I never expected to fall for a cowboy with secrets darker than a Cabernet Noir. Now, I'm caught between my growing feelings for Snapper and my guilt over my best friend's kidnapping, especially since she's his ex-girlfriend. When I insisted on joining the rescue mission, I thought I was being brave. But as we track her through Brazil's criminal underworld, I'm discovering that love and danger are a lot like wine—complex, intoxicating, and potentially deadly. The only question now is whether any of us will make it out of Brazil alive.

1
Snapper

All I could envision as I raced after the moving truck carrying what I knew were human trafficking victims was a similar scene in an action-adventure movie that had been released years before I was born. In it, the hero chased a truck—carrying the Ark of the Covenant—on horseback, like I was. He spots them from the hillside above, rides up next to the vehicle, jumps from his horse, pulls open the passenger door, grabs the first bad guy, and tosses him out, then grapples with the second guy for control of the steering wheel.

Me? All I had to do was catch up to the driver, shoot him before he shot me, then somehow prevent the truck from careening down the side of a Brazilian mountain, killing the people crammed in the back whose lives I was trying to save.

Maybe I should've thought this through before stealing the horse. Like the actor said in the movie, I was making this up as I went.

The rugged road we traveled on was to my advantage, apart from the steep drop-off unprotected by guardrails, given the horse could travel far faster than the rig could.

I remained in the driver's blind spot for as long as I could, but as soon as he spotted me—and my gun—in the side mirror, he immediately swerved, but not far enough to send me plummeting down the incline.

When he veered right and around a bend on the one-lane road, I couldn't see what was in front or to the far side of us. Clearly, he hadn't been able to, either, or wasn't paying attention in the seconds before he had a head-on collision with another vehicle.

The horse reared, nearly throwing me before I was able to jump off. Racing forward with my gun drawn, I found the driver either unconscious or dead, blood streaming from his head where it had hit the steering wheel.

"*¡Ayudame!*" I shouted to the driver of the other vehicle, motioning to the cargo area rather than at the cab. Right now, I needed help with the victims. If the driver died, so be it.

I pulled out the gun to shoot the lock off the roll-up door and shouted, "*¡Retroceder!*"—to stand back.

When I pushed the door open, the men, women, and children were huddled together, some screaming, others crying.

"*Estas seguro*," I repeated again and again, hoping my broken Spanish was close enough to their native Portuguese that they understood they were safe.

I counted twenty-four people as they piled out, many still crying and clinging to each other.

Along with not knowing how I'd stop the truck in the first place, I hadn't made a plan to transport the victims back to safety. However, I breathed a sigh of relief when I heard sirens and, moments later, vehicles displaying the *Departamento Federal de Segurança Pública* insignia drove up behind us.

My elation at their arrival was short-lived when I saw a man approaching from a truck that had parked behind them.

Marco Reis, known as *Trovão*—Thunder—in the rodeo circles we both traveled, was a world-champion bull rider. He was also the man I suspected was behind the kidnapping of the victims I'd risked my life to save.

About the Author

USA Today best-selling author Heather Slade writes shamelessly sexy, edge-of-your seat romantic suspense.

She gave herself the gift of writing a book for her own birthday one year. Sixty-plus books later (and counting), she's having the time of her life.

The women Slade writes are self-confident, strong, with wills of their own, and hearts as big as the Colorado sky. The men are sublimely sexy, seductive alphas who rise to the challenge of capturing the sweet soul of a woman whose heart they'll hold in the palm of their hand forever. Add in a couple of neck-snapping twists and turns, a page-turning mystery, and a swoon-worthy HEA, and you'll be holding one of her books in your hands.

She loves to hear from her readers. You can contact her at heather@heatherslade.com

To keep up with her latest news and releases, please visit her website at www.heatherslade.com to sign up for her newsletter.

MORE FROM AUTHOR HEATHER SLADE

BUTLER RANCH
Kade's Worth
Brodie's Promise
Maddox's Truce
Naughton's Secret
Mercer's Vow
Kade's Return
Butler Ranch Christmas

WICKED WINEMAKERS
FIRST LABEL
Brix's Bid
Ridge's Release
Press' Passion
Zin's Sins
Tryst's Temptation

WICKED WINEMAKERS
SECOND LABEL
Beau's Beloved
Cru's Crush
Bit's Bliss
Coming Soon:
Snapper's Seduction
Kick's Kiss

ROARING FORK RANCH
Roaring Fork Wrangler
Coming Soon:
Roaring Fork Roughstock
Roaring Fork Rockstar
Roaring Fork Rooker
Roaring Fork Bridger

THE ROYAL AGENTS
OF MI6
Make Me Shiver
Drive Me Wilder
Feel My Pinch
Chase My Shadow
Find My Angel

K19 SECURITY
SOLUTIONS TEAM ONE
Razor's Edge
Gunner's Redemption
Mistletoe's Magic
Mantis' Desire
Dutch's Salvation

K19 SECURITY
SOLUTIONS TEAM TWO
Striker's Choice
Monk's Fire
Halo's Oath
Tackle's Honor
Onyx's Awakening

K19 SHADOW OPERATIONS
TEAM ONE
Code Name: Ranger
Code Name: Diesel
Code Name: Wasp
Code Name: Cowboy
Code Name: Mayhem

K19 ALLIED INTELLIGENCE
TEAM ONE
Code Name: Ares
Code Name: Cayman
Code Name: Poseidon
Code Name: Zeppelin
Code Name: Magnet

K19 ALLIED INTELLIGENCE
TEAM TWO
Code Name: Puck
Code Name: Michelangelo
Code Name: Typhon
Coming Soon:
Code Name: Hornet
Code Name: Reaper

PROTECTORS
UNDERCOVER
Undercover Agent
Undercover Emissary
Undercover Savior
Coming Soon:
Undercover Infidel
Undercover Assassin

THE INVINCIBLES
TEAM ONE
Code Name: Deck
Code Name: Edge
Code Name: Grinder
Code Name: Rile
Code Name: Smoke

THE INVINCIBLES
TEAM TWO
Code Name: Buck
Code Name: Irish
Code Name: Saint
Code Name: Hammer
Code Name: Rip

THE UNSTOPPABLES
TEAM ONE
Code Name: Fury
Code Name: Merried
Coming Soon:
Code Name: Vex
Code Name: Steel
Code Name: Jagger

COWBOYS OF
CRESTED BUTTE
A Cowboy Falls
A Cowboy's Dance
A Cowboy's Kiss
A Cowboy Stays
A Cowboy Wins

Milton Keynes UK
Ingram Content Group UK Ltd.
UKHW020339031224
451863UK00013B/617